Tamburlaine's Elephants

"Beautifully written and utterly gripping...
Geraldine McCaughrean is a genius."
Philip Reeve

"I was totally captivated... I felt I was there amongst the people, the bloodshed, the revenge and the secrets."
lovereading4kids.co.uk

"McCaughrean is one of the greatest living children's authors."
The Bookseller

"McCaughrean's imagination is fierce, tireless, unpredictable."
The Observer

"McCaughrean writes every sort of book and she seems to produce them in the way a rose bush produces flowers."
The Guardian

Tamburlaine's Elephants

GERALDINE McCAUGHREAN

For Bruce Coville
and the whole "family"

Editorial consultant: Tony Bradman

First published in the UK in 2007 by Usborne Publishing Ltd.,
Usborne House, 83-85 Saffron Hill, London EC1N 8RT, England.
www.usborne.com

A CIP catalogue record for this book is available from the British Library.

JFMAMJJA OND/07

Printed in Great Britain.

Chapter One
Monsters

Rusti feared nothing but God and the lightning. Well, he was a Mongol, wasn't he? Born to a travelling life, a nomad's life. His first memories were of being cradled in the bow of a saddle, rocked to sleep by the swaying of a horse, woken by the sounds and smells of an army on the move. His life was one long journey – one long military campaign, riding in the wake of the Conqueror. Home was wherever night kissed the ground and marked the spot for pitching camp.

Rusti despised town dwellers. However magnificent the town – and in his short life he had seen many, many towns and cities – the men who lived there filled him with disgust. They were "tajiks" – stayers-in-one-place – and to a nomad all tajiks are despicable. What did they know of a warrior life? What did they know of sleeping under the stars, of riding into the teeth of a freezing wind or into the flames of battle? They were soft. They were weak. They almost asked to be conquered, as a flea asked to be squashed.

The tajiks of India did not stand a chance against Timur the Lame, Conqueror of the World. As the Chronicler Shidurghu wrote down, bending the Emir's name into a grander shape with the nib of his pen: "Tamburlaine's millions of men advanced so fast that they overtook the birds in their flight". Nothing slowed them – not their pack mules, camels, siege engines, flocks, tents, cauldrons, carts, iron baths, noise-throwing guns, travelling mosques nor their portable kitchens. Certainly not the cities that stood in their way. The Horde travelled by moonlight, storming towns and citadels by day, slaughtering thousands and taking prisoners by the tens of thousands.

Now the Conqueror's sights were set on Delhi. Listening at night to his neighbours crouched around the campfires, red-cheeked in the heat, Rusti heard them say how Delhi was a treasure house crammed with gems and perfumes, twinkling with silver, fragrant with spices. Rusti's older brother, Cokas, already had a big leather pannier full of beautiful things he had pillaged in Tiflis and Smyrna. Beneath her robes, his wife Borte rattled with silver ornaments looted on the journey south. But rumour had it that when they reached Delhi there would be the best loot of all. That's what people said.

They said Delhi had an army, too, but Tamburlaine the Great and his Mongol warriors would wash that away as a river washes away the leaves that fall into its stream. No, Rusti found nothing to fear in his young life, except for God and the lightning…

Until he reached Delhi.

Rusti pictured what he might plunder for himself when the city fell: some silver stirrups, perhaps; a rug, some jewellery for a dowry. Well? He was twelve already, wasn't he? Soon he would be old enough to marry. (Cokas had married at fourteen – though secretly Rusti was hoping for a wife less sharp-tongued than Borte, and one who made less noise when she moved.) Today nothing seemed impossible. For as of today, Rusti was old enough to ride out with the army. Rusti was old enough to be accounted a warrior!

From the ridge-top palace of Jahan-numah, the Grand Emir Tamburlaine, Lord of the Fortunate Conjunction, surveyed the Jumna river plain, seeking the ideal place to do battle with the warriors of Delhi.

If they decided to fight. Some cities just surrendered without a struggle. The people looked over the walls, saw the Mongol Horde on its way, like a tidal wave, and immediately sent ambassadors to present the symbolic shroud and sword and to beg for their lives. They wept, they implored, they grovelled and pleaded to be spared their miserable tajik lives. They emptied out their treasures at the Emir's feet, offered their sons as hostages, promised to add their soldiers to the might of Tamburlaine's army. (Occasionally, the Emir was merciful: he took their presents and allowed them to live.) In short, they were contemptible. Beetles. Ants. Fleas on the skin of the world. Rusti found it easy to despise them. After all, a man with fear in him is worth no more than a dog with worms.

The squirming heat in Rusti's own stomach was not fear – of course not! – it was the stirring of excitement. Rusti-the-Man was about to burst out from inside Rusti-the-Boy. It was no wonder he felt a little sick.

The sun was hot. Light bounced back off the baked ground like brass arrowheads: Rusti had his eyes half shut. The heat was tying side-strands of his brain into a headache. Nearby he could hear his fearsome sister-in-law rattling in her chain-mail underwear of looted spoons, brooches, ink-holders, buckles and horse bits. Maybe it was all that lumpy weight that made her scowl. Maybe she scowled at everyone like that, and not just at him. Suddenly he heard warning shouts, turned…and saw them for the first time.

Hindu cavalrymen had forayed out of the city. And with them they had brought…*monsters.* Great shapeless leather bags they were, with hideous long noses, gross, misshapen fangs, ears like flapping washing, legs like tree trunks. Their brows and chests were hung with chain mail, and castle turrets grew from their backs, big enough to hold three men. Out of these turrets flew javelins, arrows and firebombs. The fearless Mongols were thrown into panic.

The pony under Rusti went rigid. There was thunder in those trampling, monstrous feet. Blades lashed to the monsters' fangs made lightning out of the sunlight. And when they coiled back those hideous noses and bellowed, the noise was like all the demons of hell triumphing.

But it takes more than shock and horror, more than a surprise attack to unman Mongol troops. Their little cavalry ponies wheeled away down the side of the ridge, rode round the attackers and regrouped behind them. The warriors uttered shrieks quite as beasty as the monsters, and being one with their ponies, wove and darted in among the Delhi cavalry like fish among bulrushes. Short sharp scimitars delivered short sharp strokes that opened a vein, severed a rein, nicked a windpipe, or the fingers from a hand, so fast that the loser barely knew what he had lost.

Not that Rusti was among them. He was trying to regain control of his pony, which was young and had not seen battle before. It turned around and around on the spot and, when he finally persuaded it to stop, began to trot backwards sooner than move closer to the monstrous grey leather bags. Otherwise, thought Rusti, otherwise… He gnashed his teeth, rolled back his lips, and uttered a subhuman shout which, when it reached the outside of him, sounded more like a groaning bleat. Then there was a double-barrelled explosion very close to and so loud that it hurt deep inside his ears. And Rusti's pony slumped down on the spot, paralysed with fright.

The noise-throwing machines of the Horde (which had created the bang) even made Delhi's monstrous beasts halt, lean back on their haunches, flap their great ears and shriek. But that only gave the archers aboard them a steadier platform from which to fire down on the enemy. Rusti saw one arrow penetrate the helmet of a neighbour of his, and caught his breath, choking on his own spit: surely the arrow had sunk to its fletch in the man's brain? But no: it had glanced off the metal and simply slid under the fur band circling his helmet. The owner took off his helmet, grinned at his lucky escape, and jeered abuse at the archers…until another arrow hit him in the side of the throat and left him riding aimlessly about the battlefield, stone dead. To give them their due, the Hindu archers were skilled.

The tajik horsemen were good soldiers, too: emboldened by their vanguard of giant beasts, they showed courage enough and some talent for killing. But too many of the foot soldiers were ordinary citizens, undrilled, untrained, unorganized. They got under the feet of their own cavalry – even their own saggy monsters. Seeing the battle going against him, the leader of the Hindus lost his nerve and bolted for the city, his tame monsters lumbering after him. Rusti and the seven hundred would have gone after them – given chase…but for those great grey monsters bringing up the rear, shielding the retreating soldiers from attack.

As they retreated, one of the beasts tripped on the shaft of a cart and lost its footing. For agonizing moments, it teetered on two legs, then toppled sideways and rolled downhill, crushing its turret and riders. As the fleeing Hindus disappeared under a cloud of red dust, this one great land-whale lay stricken on the hillside, flailing its stumpy legs, flapping its ears, squealing like a demented pig.

No one rode in for a closer look – not until the troops parted and The Great Tamburlaine himself came cantering onto the scene. He rode round the Thing on the ground, his crippled arm folded across his stomach, his pony's hoofs dislodging pebbles. And then – wonder of wonders! – he rode back and reined in directly in front of Rusti. "What's your name, boy?"

"Rusti, Gungal Emir!"

"Then take it prisoner, Rusti. What are you waiting for? Take the beast prisoner."

"I— Yes, Gungal Emir! Right away, Gungal Emir!"

Rusti dug in his heels but his pony refused to go any closer: he had to dismount. He looked around for help, but everyone was hurrying back to camp. The men galloping past gave the monster a very wide berth indeed. Rusti was left alone with the task of getting it on its feet.

The Thing appeared helpless and worn out, so summoning up all his nerve, Rusti threw a rock at it.

When nothing happened, he ran in and kicked it. It was like kicking a boulder; for a minute he thought all his toes were broken. But the Mighty Emir, Conqueror of the World, Lord of the Fortunate Conjunction had told him to take the creature captive. Tamburlaine had given him a direct order: to take it prisoner. Desperation lent Rusti courage. He tugged on the bell-rope tail. He shoved with his shoulder against the bloated grey bulge of the belly. He even went to heave on the nose, but it groped at him like a hand, and he stepped smartly away again, out of reach.

"Aaaow!"

He had stepped back onto one of the Hindus. This was no archer or javelin thrower. He was nothing but a boy – younger even than Rusti: the driver presumably. Rusti drew his dagger. A hot, sharp pang went through him. He had just ridden into battle for the first time: now he was about to make his first kill.

Kavi the elephant boy looked up at the Mongol warrior who had trodden on him, and his throat closed up with fear. The flat round face peering down at him looked so cruel, its eastern eyes the colour of dry dust. He had heard what merciless killers these devils were, sweeping over the land like a sandstorm, leaving it scoured of life. There was no point in pleading for mercy. The only chance he stood of surviving the next few seconds was if he could rouse his elephant and make her obey him. He would command her to pick up the Mongol devil in her trunk and hurl him to the ground... Then Kavi would simply set off and run for his life...

"Get up, Mumu! Lift the devil! Toss the devil! Kill the devil!" he urged the fallen elephant.

But the elephant was dazed, hurt, afraid. She plucked at him with her trunk, like an old woman asking a neighbour's help to get up. Kavi gave a sob of frustration. Was it because of this stupid creature that he was about to die?

The boy looking up at Rusti had huge, oddly round eyes, unlike any Mongol's. His nose was bleeding, his teeth chattering with fear. Well, not a kill, perhaps. A prisoner, rather. Yes! This little elephant driver could be Rusti's first prisoner! The Great Tamburlaine had taken one hundred thousand prisoners on his march into India. Now Rusti had one of his own. It was an exciting thought. A warm feeling of power stirred in him, as the young elephant rider jabbered piteously, presumably begging for his life. But the fact remained; Rusti was supposed to make a prisoner of the elephant, too, and he had not the slightest idea how to begin.

Sudden inspiration struck. Rusti put his dagger-tip to the boy's throat, pointed at the monster and said: "Make it get up!"

A mind reader! Almost before Rusti had spoken, the little boy was up on his feet, unlashing the ruins of the turret, picking up a hooked stick, snagging the great, flapping ear, shouting at the beast in his own incomprehensible language. With a lurch, the massive animal dragged itself to its feet. Rusti could not help grinning.

"Good! Good, Mumu! Now kill him!" shouted Kavi, eye-to-eyeball with the swaying elephant. "Gore the filthy Mongol! Kill him! Do it for me!" (It did not matter how loudly he shouted it: the foreigner would not understand what he was saying.) The elephant blinked and pitched to its knees again, making both boys yelp. Kavi slapped his own skull. He sobbed and pleaded with his elephant, throat straining, failing to make the right noises of command. Soon he could not even remember the right noises to make. "Please, Mumu! Pleeeeaase! Pleeeeaaaase don't let him kill me!" he wept. At last the elephant reached out her trunk, coiled it around the thighs of the Mongol warrior and lifted him off the ground.

Rusti thought his last moment had come. He looked up into the sky, hoping to glimpse his ancestors gathering to receive his spirit. Far beneath him his prisoner's face broke into a beaming smile. Then the elephant slotted Rusti between the lumpy hills of its domed skull, and sat him gently on its neck – astride its neck. Surely he was not going to have to *ride* the monster!

With the deftness of a pickpocket, the elephant reached for the other boy and lifted him, too, onto her back. Kavi and Rusti were thrown together, the fastenings of their clothes tangled. Rusti's breath was hot and quick in Kavi's neck, making him squirm. The elephant staggered: Rusti flung his arms around the other boy's waist and clung on tight. Then Mumu took off and ran – stupid and flat-footed – heading not for home, not even for the hills, but blundering after the Mongol cavalry, bellowing like a cow in labour. Mumu was only young, and rather stupid. In fact, she was the elephant equivalent of a scared boy, caught up in his first real taste of danger.

So it was that Rusti accidentally rode into Tamburlaine's camp on the back of a war elephant, his prisoner sitting in his lap. The moment was so extraordinary that he forgot his fright. A hundred hardened warriors fell back, muttering prayers. Little children ran to their mothers. As friends of Rusti's recognized him, their mouths fell open and they pointed up at him. Neighbours struggled to put a name to his face, so that they could claim to know him: "Rusti," he heard. "Cokas's brother, Rusti." Laughter rose through Rusti as if the elephant's lumpy trot had shaken it out of him.

As for Kavi, his terror gave way to helpless despair. Wherever he looked, he saw those stitched-closed Mongol eyes. His captor's arms held his own pinned tight to his sides and the boy's laughter stirred the hairs on Kavi's neck. There would be no escape.

He was a prisoner of the Mongol Horde and his life was worth less than a fly in a jug of milk.

Rusti had to tether the beast behind a row of carts on the edge of camp, because the Mongols were so afraid of it. Even then, they moved their kibitkis as far away as possible, superstitiously whispering: "The Prince of Delhi has two hundred of these monsters!"

"Their hide is so thick no weapon can pierce it!"

"Their tusks are deadly poisonous!"

"What do they eat?"

"Small children and sheep, that's what I heard."

Rusti tethered his human prisoner, too. "Look, Cokas! I took a prisoner!" he told his brother. "The Emperor told me to fetch home the...Thing, and I did! And I've got a prisoner!"

Cokas curled his lips away from his teeth in an unattractive sneer, but there was no mistaking his surprise, his envy. He would have accused Rusti of making it up, but he had seen it with his own eyes – the Mighty Emir addressing his little brother! The boy entrusted with a man's task, and by the mighty Tamburlaine! Cokas had never so much as seen the wondrous man up close. He had never so much as seen one of these leather-bag animals before, let alone captured one.

Rusti's contempt for the little tajik lessened as he watched him pull and poke the monster about with his little hooked stick; watched him scrub its leathery back and bed down in the curl of its trunk. Next day, contempt gave way to admiration as he saw Kavi put the elephant through its paces – making it kneel, making it lie down, making it lift him bodily in its trunk, making it trumpet. The noise sent shock waves through the camp; the Mongols dropped the door-flaps of their kibitkis and sat with their fingers in their ears.

But little by little, Rusti's own terror gave way to a fascination for the hulking, gentle, sad-eyed elephant that had held him in its trunk. It had been entrusted to him by the Great Emir and, like the Emir, it filled him with awe. As with the Emir, there was no point in being afraid of it: it just was.

Watching Rusti strike up an acquaintance with *his* elephant, Kavi was jealous. But he could not help feeling a sneaking admiration for this boy, who refused to be scared of Mumu. Plainly the other Mongols were terrified of elephants, but this boy explored every inch, as if he was mapping her. He found the places where her skin got dry and sore. He found the exact place at her shoulder where she lost sight of him, because an ear got in the way. He even picked through her dung with a stick, to see the kind of things she ate.

Without ever meaning to learn each other's languages, Kavi and Rusti found they quickly understood a few words. Mahout meant elephant rider. Kibitki meant tent. In conversation, they sounded like animal trainers barking instructions. But animal-and-trainer don't laugh. Animal-and-trainer don't get the giggles. Animal-and-trainer don't experiment at wearing each other's clothes, or share their food when it is in short supply. Rather than let Rusti poke his beloved elephant with the hooked stick, Kavi showed him how to use it properly. He did so grudgingly at first, but then, seeing Rusti grin and nod and jump up and down with delight, taught him every trick, with the flourish of a magician teaching his apprentice. Before long, Rusti found that Kavi's round eyes no longer reminded him of a cow. Kavi discovered that Rusti's eastern eyes were not narrowed in disgust or hatred. In sharing rice and shelter and closeness, both boys even began to smell the same. Rather like the elephant, in fact.

Meanwhile, the citizens of Delhi continued to defy the Great Emir. They did not come out onto the Jumna Plain to fight, but neither did they surrender their treasure-house city, nor send shroud and sword, nor beg for their lives to be spared. Their defiance was heroic. It began to encourage others.

All those dejected Hindu prisoners – those one hundred thousand men, women and children Tamburlaine had captured and enslaved on his long journey of conquest – began to lift their heads. Hope stirred in their broken hearts. If the citizens of Delhi could defy Tamburlaine, perhaps *they* could recover their courage, too! Perhaps they could even rise up and break free!

Tamburlaine guessed what they were thinking. Some people sense rain coming. Tamburlaine sensed what was in the minds of his one hundred thousand prisoners. He had not captured half the world by using gentleness and generosity. He had not rolled up the maps of Asia and put them in his pocket using kindliness and pity. It is ruthlessness that makes for conquest. Now his ruthlessness uncoiled like the lash of a whip. He knew how to thwart an uprising.

"Kill them all," he told his men. "Kill all the prisoners."

It does not take minutes. It does not take hours. It takes whole days to kill one hundred thousand men, women and children. Whole days and nights. Isolated from the rest of the vast, sprawling camp, Rusti, Kavi and the elephant listened to the massacre being carried out.

One thousand acres of screaming.

One thousand acres awash with blood.

One thousand acres of twisted bodies and gathering flies.

The noises scoured Rusti's head empty of thought. Mumu heaved herself from foot to foot, her great head tossing from side to side. Long after dark she kept up her dance of distress.

Rusti knew that he, like everyone else, must kill his prisoners. But how? One – the elephant – he did not know *how* to kill. The other – his friend – he did not… know how to kill, either. It was a different kind of ignorance – he hated himself for it – told himself he was a man now and that men know how to do these things. But nightfall came and still he havered, irresolute. Kavi stared at him, dumb with terror, awash with tears, the elephant's trunk caressing his small face, as if trying to read its expression in the dark.

"Kavi dead?" said Kavi, and the knees of his twiggy little legs knocked together in spasms of terror.

Rusti took out his dagger and studied it. It lay across the palm of his hand, the same shape as an elephant's tusk. As he moved towards Kavi, he saw the boy's legs sag and his head turn towards the darkness of the open plain. "Don't run," said Rusti.

Of course some of the prisoners had broken free of their executioners and fled – run and limped and hopped and crawled out onto the plain, gasping for breath, pelting towards the distant lights of Delhi. Tomorrow the cavalry would ride out, overtaking and cutting them down one by one, finishing off the task set them by the Grand Emir. Out on the plain there was nowhere to hide.

"Don't run," said Rusti.

Kavi drew his arms across his body, eyes fixed on the knife in Rusti's hand. Of course he could always fight – fight Rusti for the knife and try to wrest it from him: be the killer and not the killed.

As if he had read Kavi's thoughts, Rusti suddenly thrust the knife back into his belt, ducked down and picked up the long, hooked stick they both used for controlling Mumu. Kavi's arms rose to protect his head: so he was to be cudgelled to death, was he? Beyond the row of carts the massacre went on, torchlit shadows leaping huge and ghastly. Kavi shut his eyes – and felt Rusti brush up against him. Mumu gave a grunt.

Rusti had poked her with the hooked stick – had jabbed it into the elephant's ear, in fact, and brought her to her knees. Now he tapped Kavi on the shoulder and gave a twitch of his head: "Get on," he said.

Kavi's large eyes glistened in the darkness; it was all Rusti could make out of his friend's face. Kavi crouched down, kissed Rusti's foot, then scrambled onto the elephant's knee, up onto her head. Elephant and mahout swayed away into the dark: elephants can move at tremendous speed when they choose.

Rusti did not watch them go; he was too busy dragging all the elephant's dung into a pile, covering it with straw, setting it alight.

When Tamburlaine called for all the severed heads of his one hundred thousand prisoners to be piled up in cairns, Rusti explained that he had had to burn the elephant (and its mahout), there being no other way to kill it. He pointed out a large, grey, smoking heap as proof. Even the skulls had burned, he said.

Knowing nothing of elephants, no one questioned it. They believed what Rusti told them.

Chapter Two

Taking Delhi

When Delhi finally opened its gates and loosed its army of living weapons, the elephants made a terrifying sight in their chain mail. Fire, javelins and arrows rained down from their turreted howdahs.

But elephants are not indestructible, of course, and their tusks are not poisonous. They do not eat children or small animals. Tamburlaine the Great had had time to think. Thanks to that little elephant-capturing warrior – what was his name? – Tamburlaine had worked out a way to fight this elephant cavalry corps. He ordered bundles of dried grass to be tied to the backs of camels and buffaloes and set alight. Then the burning animals were stampeded in among the elephants.

Rusti watched, spellbound with horror. He peered through the smoke, trying to tell Mumu from the other elephants, trying to spot Kavi. It was as if Rusti had had the idea and the Great Emir had carried it through: to burn Mumu, to burn Kavi before his very eyes. As the abominable stench reached him on the wind, he was glad of the stinging smoke that accompanied it: he could blame the smoke for the tears that poured shamingly down his cheeks.

In their terror, the elephants turned and trampled their own Hindu troops. Mongols scaled their grey backs, and hacked down the castle howdahs; Mongol axes slashed through the swinging trunks. Any surviving elephants were taken prisoner.

So the city of Delhi fell, just as Constantinople, Tashkent, Kabul, Tiflis and Astrakhan had fallen before it. In went Tamburlaine and his Mongols, angry at being kept waiting so long for their plunder.

Among them was Rusti, on his first pillaging raid. To enter the city, they had to ride around the fallen, the wounded, the horses, the burning howdahs, the screaming buffaloes, the dying camels. Rusti did not look. He kept his eyes straight ahead, fixed on the City of Gems.

"Keep close to me," said his brother, "and keep

away from the buildings – the tajiks will try to drop things on your head. Watch out for archers on the roofs."

Perhaps there were fabulous treasures found in the Delhi palaces? If so, they went to the Emir's Royal Guard and the seasoned warriors. They knew how to penetrate in minutes to the heart of a falling city; how to thwart the pitiful attempts of the tajiks to hide their riches and finery; how to beat their fellow Mongols to the loot. But warriors should move fast, if they want a share of the spoils. It was all new to Rusti. He dawdled, cautiously watching every window and rooftop, trying to take in the size, beauty and squalor of the city. So of course he was left with nothing to loot but trinkets and everyday dross: leatherware and cheap jewellery. He took a sword from a dead man, but the blade was bent. He looted himself some spices, but the bag snagged on the bent sword and split, staining him from head to foot in yellow and red and green dust. The mixed smells made his head spin. Every house seemed to have been pillaged by the time he got there – disembowelled, spilling its guts into the street, along with some dead old man or child or dog. Cows, looking stupid and puzzled, clogged up the streets. Rusti had not been expecting cows.

His brother was furiously irritated by him. "We'll get nothing! We are getting nothing!" he raged. "You are so slow! I hope Borte has done better than us!" Somewhere ahead of them, his wife too was marauding through the alleyways of Delhi, blue scarf drawn up over her nose, eyes glaring fiercely enough to light fires among the rubble and rubbish.

So the brothers turned aside down a steep, stepped alleyway, in the hope of finding some untouched source of booty. A man in a turban ran out into their path, waving his hands in the air, wanting to surrender. Rusti's brother rode him down.

Rusti felt a scorching pain as a badly aimed arrow scuffed his back and hit the wall beside him, with a pinging noise. His brother wrested his pony's head round, came back at the gallop and threw a burning brand in at a doorway, judging it to be the house sheltering the archer. Maybe it was. Maybe it wasn't.

At the bottom of the steep slope, the lane grew so narrow they could not even turn their ponies around, and there was no way forward: only a dead end blocked by a big wooden barn. Behind them, the fire started by Cokas's brand was spreading quickly to the other houses, and tajiks were emerging from hiding to keep from being burned alive. Some were trying to save their children or their belongings. Others were armed.

"Your fault," Rusti's brother told him, leaning out of his saddle, wrenching open the door of the barn. Sinking his heels into his pony's flanks, he made it lurch forward into the darkness of the rickety building.

Rusti heard Cokas cry out, the pony shriek, the thud of a rider hitting the ground. His own pony stumbled and he went over its head – spilled head-over-heels into the darkness of the big space.

And there was Mumu.

It was Mumu and it was not. Even those great flapping ears had not been able to shut out the sounds of Tamburlaine's three-day massacre. The smells of the atrocity had sheathed themselves in that great flexing nose. By the time Kavi had ridden her back, at full tilt, from the Mongol camp to the gates of Delhi, she was a shuddering, prancing, cribbing, wild thing. Mumu was out of her wits.

When the armourers had come to prepare her for battle – bind blades to her tusks, strap on her howdah, clothe her in link mail, she had simply stood with her rump in the corner of the barn, prancing her front feet, rolling blood-red eyes and bellowing threats to trample them. Cursing her, cursing her little mahout, they had shut her up in the darkness of the barn before going out to do battle with Tamburlaine.

Now Mumu greeted the sunlight like glass underfoot. She had felled Cokas's pony, picked up Cokas in her trunk and thrown him against the wall. Now she coiled her trunk and turned her head, three-quarters on, to eye the figure scrambling to its feet in the doorway. Then one tusk scraped through the dirty straw like a ploughshare through soil, and she came at Rusti, grotesquely crouching and twisted, her head on one side, front legs splayed, back legs charging.

Rusti needed his brother now, big and strong and brave. But Cokas lay unconscious in a pile of dung, at the foot of the wall. Rusti needed his legs to run, but they were waiting for his heart to beat again, and it had forgotten how.

"Mumu. Stand." Small and sharp as a mosquito, a little-boy voice came out of the rafters. Kavi's little-boy form dropped onto the elephant's back – astride her contorted shoulders where the hide had folded into prodigious wrinkles. "Mumu. Stand." His mahout's stick swung and poked: same shape as a mosquito's sting. How could such a tool possibly subdue a beast as huge and frenzied as a mad cow-elephant? "Mumu. Stand."

Mumu turned her head so sharply that her flaccid trunk lashed sideways, heavy as hawser, and knocked Rusti to the ground – knocked all the wind out of him. When he looked up, all he could see was the pointed bottom lip of the elephant, and the great spreading arcs of her twin tusks. "Mumu," he said, but had no breath to put behind the word and give it sound.

Then something damp and hollow and fluted and warm and terrifying settled over his face. It sucked his cheek from between his teeth. It sucked the hair from behind his ear. It sucked the mucous from his nose, the blood from the cut on his forehead.

Mumu ran the fluted tip of her trunk over Rusti's face like a blind man reading a frieze.

Then one, two, three, four: her feet stepped over him and she moved up the narrow alleyway, grazing her sides against the house walls, impervious to the tufts of flame and plumes of smoke scorching her delicate hide. Kavi, crouching up on her spine on hands and knees to look back the way he had come, met Rusti's eyes and spoke.

"Butchers," he said. "All savages and butchers."

The words were spoken in a foreign tongue, and though each boy had picked up a little of the other's language, Rusti did not understand. He thought he could guess the meaning of the words. He thought Kavi must have called, *"Friends. Friends for ever, no matter what!"* After the fighting, after the plundering, after the victory, he would search out Kavi among the prisoners. Not difficult, after all: a boy on an elephant is hard to miss.

After the fall of Delhi, the Great Emir Tamburlaine set up his pavilion at one of the city gates and accepted the surrender of the city's noblemen, scholars and officials. Musicians played. Poets improvised victory verses in praise of the man who had captured, looted and mangled the City of Gems. As he listened, a thought occurred to the Conqueror of the World and he leaned sideways in his golden chair and spoke a command into the ear of a messenger. The messenger paled and bit his lip.

"The elephants! I have to bring the elephants!" cried the messenger, eyes hot with panic. He came clambering over the wagons in search of Rusti, raising one arm as he did so, to try and shut out the sight of the captured elephants of Delhi. "The Mighty Emir wants them to parade before him! But how? We killed all the riders!"

"All of them?" said Rusti stupidly. His hands were full of hay. He had been given charge of the sorry, injured, frightened, captured elephants and he had been trying to calm them and bed them down before dark.

"Yes, yes!"

"No prisoners? There aren't *any* mahouts among the prisoners?"

The messenger's eyes bulged with frustration. "That's what I said, didn't I? So what to do? What to do? *What to do?"* The Emir's temper clearly frightened him even more than the elephants.

"I will bring them," said Rusti.

Tamburlaine, his maimed arm and leg more evident out of the saddle, surveyed his conquest from a chair in the doorway of his crimson pavilion. Rhinoceroses from the Sultan of Delhi's zoo came trampling past – gross, baggy unicorns whose heads took up a third of their bodies. Whipped to a waddle, they passed by the Emir's throne, silent, sullen, averting their small, piggy eyes. Their indifference irritated and offended Tamburlaine. The dark, mustard-coloured hands resting on the arms of the gilded wooden throne twitched and clenched with dissatisfaction. The courtiers to either side of him quailed and hunched their shoulders. Every day the Emir's temper grew more unpredictable, more terrifying.

Then the elephants were brought out – sorry, tattered elephants blotched with their own blood. They were being led by a boy not above twelve years old. The victorious crowds shrank back involuntarily, but the boy seemed to have no fear of the great, shapeless giants. And he was not even an Indian mahout, but a Mongol, just like them! A young boy, barely old enough to have seen battle! And yet he hoicked and prodded each in turn until, one by one, the elephants slumped to their knees.

Tamburlaine slid to the front of his throne. "They are kneeling to me!" he cried delightedly.

Rusti drove his stick into the leathery hide, spoke a single soft word, and the elephants threw up their heads and bellowed – a noise like a thousand triumphant trumpets. A look of rapture crossed the Emir's face, which Rusti felt in his own breast and which he would never forget.

"They salute me! The monsters are saluting me!" cried the Emir, his voice childlike and piping. The small boy steering the elephants might as well have been invisible, for the Emir saw only the giants dancing, not their dance master. But the court officials to right and left of the throne stopped wringing their hands. They caught Rusti's eye, their faces full of gratitude – even admiration. They could not have done so much. They could not have got the better of these monumental grey satchels of wrinkled hide. They could not have put such a smile on the weather-beaten face of the Emir Tamburlaine, Lord of the Fortunate Conjunction.

Last in the string of elephants came Mumu, smaller than the rest and with a nervous, sidling gait. She had been found wandering vacantly among the ruined palaces of Delhi, one tusk shattered, her trunk kinked like a cat's tail that has been shut in a door. She was utterly docile. Rusti understood why now: Mumu had despaired. He had seen that same silent stillness in the mothers and widows of Delhi, who had lost their sons and brothers and husbands and city. Just from the sagging hopelessness of her head, Rusti knew that Mumu had lost Kavi.

Like all the other elephants, Mumu kneeled to

Tamburlaine. She too bellowed his praises to the purpling evening sky. Rusti was almost disappointed in her. Then he remembered that he did not speak Elephant very well yet. Perhaps, after all, Mumu was bellowing filthy, defiant curses at the Gungal Emir, threatening revenge. Perhaps all of the elephants were kneeling there thinking, "One swipe of my trunk, and I could wipe that smile off your face, Gungal Emir, quicker than you could say, *'I win'*." It was a shocking thought and Rusti wondered whatever had put it into his head.

The Chronicler Shidurghu, recorder of the mighty deeds of Tamburlaine, wrote down how the Lord of the Fortunate Conjunction had conquered Delhi as the lion conquers the gazelle, as the sun conquers night, as the sickle conquers the wheat. In his beautiful tooled leather book he listed the treasures that had been captured and shared out among the Horde. He wrote what great mercy the Emir had shown to those who surrendered – of the justice meted out to those who had defied his might. Shidurghu wrote of the outlandish animals that had paraded past the royal throne; how the elephants had trumpeted their praise for the Gungal Emir. But if Shidurghu wrote in his chronicle about the young

Mongol boy who had *tamed* the fearful giants, he did not mention it to Rusti. Boys like Rusti do not learn to read, let alone glimpse History on the page.

CHAPTER THREE

THE SPOILS OF WAR

Mumu was not the only one to have been injured in the taking of the city. Rusti's brother Cokas remembered nothing about the looting of Delhi. Rusti had managed to drag him out of the barn, through the elephant dung and dirty straw, just as the thatch caught light. Somehow he had managed to put Cokas face down across his horse, but all the way home, his face had slapped limply against the horse's flank. He was still unconscious when they got back to camp, and did not come round until after the victory parade and the speeches of surrender. While Rusti was putting the elephants through their paces in front of the Great Emir, Cokas lay like a dead man in his tent.

Where Mumu had thrown him against the wall, a patch of his hair had been torn off and his skull dented. In the days that followed, he drifted up to the surface of sleep and asked questions, demanded answers. But then he would sink back down, so deeply asleep, that, from time to time, Borte had to turn him over with the sole of her foot, to stop him choking on his own tongue.

"Wake up, man! Get up!" she would bark, her voice as sharp as a cheap enamelled dagger. "They are dividing up the cattle! They are dividing up the spoil! We are missing out!" The fact that Rusti had been awarded a slave-girl and fifty gold coins, by order of the Emir, seemed to enrage, not comfort, her.

A slave-girl? When Rusti first heard this, he was delighted. A slave-girl to fetch and carry for him, to fold up his bed and pack his belongings, to pour him a cup of water, to saddle his horse and cure the skins of the animals he caught when he went hunting! A slave-girl to mend his clothes for him and pick the lice out of his hair! But as he approached the acre of wailing women and children corralled on the plain, delight gave way to doubt. Would he have to *feed* her, this slave-girl he had won? Where was she supposed to sleep? Should he choose one big enough to do all his work, or one smaller than him, so that he could safely beat her without her hitting him back?

When he saw them, he stopped thinking and just stared. Here were the *real* gems of Delhi – these slim-bodied women with liquid eyes like deer and dark waterfalls of glossy hair. Their tissuey brightness was torn and streaked with dirt where, in their grief, they had rent at their clothing and daubed themselves with dust or soot. From time to time one would bend down and scrape at the parched ground and rub the dirt into her shining black hair. Jewellery had been torn from delicate noses and ears, leaving streaks of blood. Dusky children clasped their mothers' legs. Old women sat on the ground, silently rocking, covering their faces with big-knuckled hands.

Rusti felt a pain, as if a runaway goat had butted him in the stomach. He could not understand why, and wondered for a moment if he had eaten something rotten. Why else would his stomach cramp and the sickness gather in his throat?

How to choose? It was one thing to pick a pony from amongst a captured herd. It was different to pick out a girl. Would the Emir be offended if he refused the honour? (Would Borte ever forgive him?)

A cordon of warriors encircled the widows and

orphans of Delhi. Now and then one would lunge forward and, plucking a captive by the wrist, drag her away to his kibitki, or give her his shield to carry or tie her plait to his bridle. Children were separated from their mothers. The air was full of shrieking and sobbing. Rusti told himself these were tajiks, and did not feel things as keenly as Mongol women and children. They would soon get used to slavery. But somehow the noise and fluttering tatters of the prisoners made the pain worse and worse under his belt. He found himself wishing the Mighty Tamburlaine had overlooked him when it came to doling out rewards.

I will choose one who's quiet and won't cry all the time, he decided, and began to search among the faces for just one girl who was dry-eyed. That was when he saw Kavi.

Astonishing that he recognized the little mahout at all, under the drapery of a woman's sari, little clenched fists half hiding his face. But the huge round eyes were fixed on Rusti, and there was something in the look – that mixture of shame and terror and pleading – that snatched Rusti's attention and put the name right there in his mouth: "Kavi?" He wanted to laugh.

Men were pushing through the huddle of women and girls, just as they had waded into the lily ponds of Delhi's palaces to wrench up the lilies. They pulled back shawls, flicked hanks of hair, felt what strength was in an arm – even checked the captives' teeth, as they would ponies at a horse fair. At any moment, a hand would fall on Kavi, strip away his disguise and show him for what he was: a frightened gibbering little boy trying to save his wretched hide by pretending to be a girl. A Mongol warrior would die rather than do such a thing, but Delhi boys (Rusti told himself) could hardly be expected to be forged from the same iron.

A pair of brothers, who had been drinking for hours, lurched out of a nearby kibitki and into the compound, peering blearily about. Without each other to lean on, neither could have kept upright, but leaning shoulder-against-shoulder they ploughed their way through the prisoners, determined not to let the best spoils of war escape them. One pointed at Kavi – "Her! Shkinny chicken with the big eyes!" – then both ducked their heads and plunged towards him, huge and noisy. If Rusti hesitated one moment longer, his friend's life would slip out of his grasp, into a bottomless ravine, and those round eyes would haunt his nightmares for ever. The brothers parted, like the flaps of a tent, intending to pinion Kavi between them. Rusti darted right between them and grabbed Kavi by both wrists. "This one's mine," he said.

One drunken brother seemed inclined to punch Rusti in the face, but the other recognized him – "'S'elephantboy!" – and they beamed generously at him and lurched off to rumple and paw a few more of the gems of Delhi.

Without a word, Rusti pushed Kavi ahead of him, wanting to say his name, wanting to giggle at the sari, at the situation; at the same time knowing that it was not funny, not one bit funny. Kavi said nothing, but held his lips between his teeth and stumbled and rounded his shoulders and folded his hands in against his body and sobbed once or twice out of purest fear. *I should tell someone*, thought Rusti, knowing already that he would not.

Surely his brother and sister-in-law were bound to recognize Kavi as soon as they saw him? After all, before the fall of Delhi, before the massacre of prisoners, Rusti and the little mahout had been together every day. What if they accused him of helping an enemy? What would he say then? He would say he had not *noticed* the captive was a boy! Ah, but then he would be laughed to scorn! Rusti hesitated outside the tent, jigging from foot to foot. Oh for an elephant. With an elephant under him, he was a warrior who commanded respect. Without an elephant, he was just a boy. Grabbing one of Kavi's wrists roughly, he lifted the tent flap and went in.

"What did you get?" Borte snapped at him. She was pushing a lump of mutton about a pot of boiling water as if it was still alive and she trying to drown it. "No one worth having, I'll swear."

"Hold your tongue, woman," said a voice from his bed in the deep dark shadows of the tent. Cokas was conscious again. "It's a fool who spits on good luck."

Always a superstitious man, Cokas had taken it into that dented skull of his that his little brother Rusti had been blessed with good luck by the ancestors: something he had dreamed, perhaps. Now Cokas flapped one hand, summoning the slave-girl to come closer so that he could look "her" over.

Rusti gave Kavi a push. "She's called Kavita," he told his brother.

Kavi tottered into the darkness as towards a lion in its den. After the bright sunshine, his eyes could make out nothing, but gradually the deeper darkness at his feet resolved itself into a pile of animal skins and the figure of a man, his head swathed in dirty bandages. The eyes seemed shineless, dead: pain had crumpled up Cokas's face, like a sheet of vellum.

Though it cost him tremendous effort, Cokas swivelled his eyes towards the shape. It was silhouetted against the knifing sunlight in the doorway, and he did not want to admit that he could see two, three, four overlapping slave-girls. "Passable," he said. "She's passable."

Rusti waited for his sister-in-law to recognize Kavi – to shriek – to laugh? – to demand an explanation. Her fists closed around Kavi's upper arm and she jerked him towards the daylight. Her eyes flicked over him from head to foot, and what she saw brought a sneer to her flat leathery face. Then she went back to the cooking pot and sank the mutton so violently that the broth slopped out over her feet. "More meat on a locust," she said, and she did not mean the mutton bone.

She saw what she expected to see: a captive tajik in a dress. Who troubles to look at a tajik's face anyway? They all look the same.

* * *

"It is all right! You see? You see?" said Rusti, the first time the two boys were truly alone. They had gone to tend the elephants, and the elephants guaranteed they would be on their own. "See Mumu? There's Mumu! Right there! She knows you, I'm sure she does. You know Kavita, don't you, Mumu! No one is going to kill you, Kavita! You can help me with the elephants. If you want, I'll say you have to stay here and sleep with the elephants at night, and Borte will never suspect, and people don't dare come near here, and it'll be like before…"

The huge round eyes looked back at him, blankly. Kavi said not a word, but went and stood on the far side of an elephant, stroking the grey hide with small grey hands, tracing the maze of grey wrinkles with the tip of one finger.

Rusti was too glad to notice. He had an ally in the world again – someone who did not scowl at him, someone who did not expect him simply to kill things and to get drunk; someone who was more scared than he was. (Oh, the joy of finding there was someone in the world who was more scared than he was!) With his big eyes and his rustling, female clothes, "Kavita" was in no position to condemn Rusti for being soft, for still secretly feeling like a little boy on the inside. Rusti was too glad to notice: Kavi said nothing at all.

If Kavi had been thrown from a boat in mid ocean, then to stay alive he would have learned to swim. Different skills were needed here, but he had to learn them just as fast. Here, it was a matter of learning to walk with a sway of the hips and never taking long strides; of tilting his head forward and keeping his eyes on the ground; of guessing the meaning of the words shouted at him; of doing everything he was told; of rising before dawn and spending as much of the day as possible among the elephants, where he was left in peace and where Borte would not come looking to hit him.

Kavita's hair already reached his shoulder blades. Because it was coarser than a girl's, Rusti combed sesame oil into it, and so his slave-girl took on a scent much sweeter than elephant (or elephant boy). Most wisely of all, Kavita never spoke. Not that Kavi's voice had broken, or had anything very masculine about it. But by not speaking, he escaped attention. At first Borte would hit out with whatever she was holding – bridle, ladle, tent pole, fist – whenever

Kavita came within range. But when the slave-girl's soft and silent comings and goings did not disturb her daily routines, Borte almost forgot about Kavita. Kavi was a quick learner too. Every day he learned a dozen new words, an oath or two.

In fact, Kavi was a natural born actor. He played his part to perfection, learning the lines, studying the moves. Soon the feminine gestures and movements became second nature to him. So did the loathing he felt for himself.

Chapter Four

Rain

Amazingly, the disguise went on working! Cokas was too ill to notice anything. His neighbours were too absorbed in their own ever-shifting lives. Even Borte still did not see through the lie. Maybe she scowled so much that those shaggy eyebrows of hers blinded her.

The patch of hair torn from Cokas's skull never regrew. In the weeks that followed, his skin took on a waxy paleness and his face thinned, so that his teeth looked too big for his mouth. Food made him sick. It was a problem. It was a problem during the weeks the Horde spent stripping Delhi, like eagles stripping a carcass. It was more of a problem once the Horde stirred itself and moved on.

Rain

Every morning Cokas had to be got onto his horse; helped into the saddle; handed his own reins. But inside his dented head, little night-times would fall without warning, and then he would tumble out of the saddle and hit the ground without so much as putting out a hand to save himself. So they put him into a cart, cocooned in his bedding, wedged in with the bulky folds of the family kibitki. Each time a wheel struck a rock or dropped into a rut, Cokas would be pitched about, rolling from side to side, groaning and cursing. Borte told Kavita to ride in the cart with him, and so Kavi sat with Cokas's head in his lap, while the tossing of the cart flexed his spine like a whip. Kavi's world shrank to a lapful of greasy hair, a mouthful of stinking breath, an open head-wound.

Rusti, riding astride the largest of the elephants, leading the others, could look down into the cart where his friend and his brother rode. He too watched Cokas sink and shrink and turn into a different sort of brother – one who needed help to eat, one who mumbled and squealed, one who saw things when they were not there.

It was dismal travelling at the rear. The dust that rose up from the heels of the vast, migrating army quickly coated Rusti and the elephants and the cart and its occupants so thickly that they looked like earthenware statues. Borte, who was used to riding among the foremost five hundred, alongside her warrior husband, could not endure to be among the pack mules and the baggage wagons and the captured elephants. The sight of Cokas babbling to himself, his head in the lap of a slave-girl, was even more intolerable than the tons of dust settling on her head. Prestige came from being married to a warrior, but none from being saddled with a sick and useless idiot. But though she shrieked this in Cokas's face several times a day, he still refused to pull himself together. Borte rode alongside the cart for a week or so, then moved farther and farther ahead.

Rusti would have liked to ride with her – well, not *with* her, perhaps, but farther forward, up among the warriors. He was, after all, a warrior himself. He and the elephants ought to be leading the way, dwarfing the puny cavalrymen on their fighting ponies, keeping a lookout for ambushers and guerrillas and the dust cloud that would signal the approach of a massed army. Inside his head, Rusti imagined himself charging into battle, acquitting himself like a hero, taking Cokas's place, slashing to right and left, firing arrows point-blank into the faces of oncoming…

Rain

Plash, plash. Cold drops fell in his face and cut canals through the caked mask of dust.

Then the rains came.

The noise of thunder had been making everybody jittery for days. Rusti was not alone in fearing lightning: the whole Mongol Horde went in terror of thunderstorms. Thunder spoke of a restless heaven, of angry ancestors. So warriors and courtiers alike were a-jump with nerves when, with a noise like the sky collapsing, the monsoon rains came.

Drops fell in sharp, hard grains the size of rice – then huge eggy globules; then gouts as warm as blood; then torrents so dense that the ancestors must have been emptying pails of water out of the sky.

In fact poor, sick Cokas thought he could *see* the ancestors doing it.

The lice in Rusti's hair took shelter under his chin, then in his armpits, then in his groin. Then they were sluiced away altogether, along with packs from the horses, pipes from belts, food from the wagons, trees from the hills. The dust washed off. The elephants changed colour, to a dark granite grey, and tassels of water hung from their tails and sprayed from the tips of their swinging trunks as they walked.

In the space of a day, dry river valleys turned into

roaring torrents of water bearing along whole trees and bushes and drowned animals. Tracks turned to slicks of mud more slippery than ice. The scenery disappeared – whole mountains, whole plains – behind a curtain of falling water, so that the army slowed to a halt, the ponies turning round and round on the spot, disorientated, struggling to keep their footing. Horsemen cursed their mounts for refusing to budge, drummed their feet into the ponies' ribs and drove them forward, only to find the ponies had had a reason for stopping dead: the ground ahead was not solid. So mud came up to their boots – to their sword hilts – to their chests – to their necks… Unable to back out or reach firm ground, they kept on moving forwards. Rusti watched men ride into mud up to their eyes – and then a helmet was floating for a moment – and then it was gone.

Rusti had never seen men ride underground before.

The mighty Tamburlaine was sheltered from the downpour by a canopy over his head; four outriders held the four corner poles. But the outriders' eyelids were beaten shut by the raindrops. The poles grew so slippery, their hands so cold and wet, the canopy so heavy with rain, that one pole broke and the canopy slipped, dumping a bathful of water onto the head of the Gungal Emir, Conqueror of the World.

The outriders, seeing that nothing but death awaited, rode off into the rain and instantly disappeared from sight. It was as if the ancestors had passed judgement and dissolved them into mud.

Mud. It rose up over the wheels of the siege engines. It flowed into the throats of the noise-throwing guns. It desecrated the portable mosques. It gulped down the portable kitchens. Sheep and goats, lifted from their feet, floated by – bleating, capsizing – and sank from sight. The pack mules brayed in dismay at the disappearance of their hoofs, their knees, at the cold slop of mud against their bellies. Their eyes rolled. Their packs floated away. Camels stood stock still amid the chaos, like stilt huts in a brown lake.

Rusti, in charge of the elephants, feared every moment that they would take fright and stampede. He badly wanted Kavi's help, and peered through the blinding rain for the cart. At his first clear sight of Kavita, his heart gave a lurch of fear. For the rain had turned the thin clothing transparent and plastered it against the thin body inside. It was plain, to anyone with eyes, that Kavita was a boy.

But nobody was looking. Nobody had time for so much as a glance: they had troubles enough of their own. A cartload of kibitkis had just overturned and the skin tents were sinking into the swill, like pigs drowning.

The bull elephants answered the thunder with defiant bellows. The smaller, female elephants began to scamper in circles or nod their heads up and down, up and down, like gossips fervently agreeing with one another.

"Kavita! Kavita! Come and help me! Come and ride Altan!"

Kavi looked up, his long eyelashes full of glistening rain. With a slight tilt of his head, he indicated that he had already been given his task for the day: to look after the injured Cokas. In his lap, Cokas was thrashing about, open hands slapping the hides that cradled him, talking to invisible people:

"Look there, see? Jebe come down, you'll fall! Rusti tell him. Hey look! Buji is puking again! He eats too much cheese, that one! Temujin – hey Temujin!! Have you seen my dog? It was here…before… I had it right here in the…"

Rusti put his fingers in his ears. Kavi scowled up at him, not understanding.

"Don't you hear? My brother is naming dead people! Everyone knows! You must *never, never, never* speak the names of the Dead! It brings disaster!" But worse than hearing his brother speak the unspeakable was knowing that Cokas plainly *was* seeing the ancestors – that they really were there – amid all this chaos – flying blithely through rain so torrential it was bringing horses to their knees.

The ancestors were gathering like crows over a battlefield.

Dread seized Rusti. "Kavita! Kavita! Make him be quiet! Do something!"

Bewildered, Kavi put his fingers into Cokas's babbling mouth, and winced as the man chewed on them.

The elephants, who had seen many a monsoon, were quite untroubled by the rain. But they did begin to pick up on the human terror around them. They mooed and twirled and tossed their heads. Rusti shouted commands at them, but such was the hiss of the rain, even he could not hear what came out of his own mouth. A little bull calf elephant suddenly turned and ran off. Within a few strides, it was lost from sight – rubbed out by the rain. It would wreak havoc among the baggage wagons.

"Come and help me, Kavi! Please!"

Kavi squirmed out from under Cokas, whose thrashing arm caught him a blow on the ear. Cokas went on grinning at the faces he saw in the sky, calling up to them: "Khasar! Thought you were dead, my friend! Stop spilling your drink on me, Khasar, you clumsy dog!"

Kavi hitched up his skirts and clambered up onto the beast alongside Rusti's, and they steered all the elephants away from the chaotic column of men, women, children, carts, animals and machines. Terrifyingly, a rhinoceros appeared out of the blinding rain, at one point, and trotted clear between them, its wrinkled hide streaming. The Emir's zoo was escaping under cover of the rainstorm.

For a mile or more the elephant boys encountered clusters of people, overturned carts, tents pitched by those who had decided to sit out the rain and hide from the lightning. Invisible one moment, people suddenly appeared right in the path of the trotting elephants – blurred figures seized by panic, scrabbling to get out of the way, snatching up children and baskets... Kavi had to get the elephants far, far away from the floundering Horde.

Not that the Horde was a column, walking single

file, of course – nothing as organized as an army. It was a nation strung out from one horizon to the other. But Kavi and Rusti struck off at a tangent and somehow, eventually, reached somewhere free of people; where there seemed to be nothing but rain and mud and thunder. They plodded blindly through a monsoon that turned the sky green and washed away the horizon. It washed the thoughts out of their heads, the words out of their mouths. They just rode.

The rain would slacken from time to time, raising Rusti's hopes...then new downpours pulsed across the sky. Noon and evening were indistinguishable. Grey trees stood in the murk, like giant ghosts. Rusti was a Mongol, a herd animal. To him, solitude like this was as menacing as a pack of wolves.

"I think we should turn back now," he said at last. "Find Borte. Find Cokas."

Kavi said nothing.

"Did *you* see them?" Rusti blurted out.

"See?" said Kavi, speaking for the first time.

"The ancestors! My brother could see the ancestors!" Rusti said, frightening himself all over again. "He spoke their names. That's bad luck a million times over!"

"He die," said Kavi with a shrug, and found that the thought gave him pleasure.

"Die? No! Ha-ha! Cokas isn't dying! He's a warrior! Hard like a rock!"

Kavi shrugged again. "People die. All people. Is will of God." But he found that it was also the will of Kavita. Kavita wished Cokas dead, along with his ugly wife and all his kind. "I go now. I go home."

"What? NO!"

But Kavi's elephant had broken into a trot. The dark, gleaming slab of grey, the smear of bright colours astride its neck was moving off at speed. Kavi, like the captured animals, was making a bid for freedom.

Elephants are herd animals: the rest set off to follow, despite Rusti cursing them and ordering them to come back.

Kavi urged on Deepti – a big cow-elephant who seemed just as eager as he was to escape slavery. In fact, she willingly broke into a run.

"Come back, Kavi!" called Rusti, and in his surprise and fright, he shouted all the wrong things, all the worst things he could have said:

"I saved you!

Where can you go?

I forbid you!

I own you!

You're my slave-girl!

I won you!"

Soon the two boys were riding at full tilt – clinging tight – Kavi shouting over his shoulder, "Go away! Go back!" –

Rusti taking no notice – "Wait! Don't go!"

Thunder rumbled around the sky. Water splashed from under the flat-footed elephants. Then a whole muddle of dark hummocks, like molehills, were suddenly cluttering up their path...

Tents.

And mothers were running to snatch small children out of the way, and there were dogs, and banners flapping, and hobbled ponies rearing up in panic. Kavi tried to slow down, but Deepti did not stop running. She had not taken off in search of freedom at all. She was looking for her calf – the one that had run off during the storm – and she did not stop running until she found him.

Unwittingly, the elephant boys had ridden full circle and returned to the Horde. Kavi broke down and wept; the rain bullied the tears off his face.

* * *

Deepti was reunited with her calf. Rusti was reunited with his sister-in-law and her rattling armour of cutlery and bad temper. Tamburlaine was reunited with his prize string of war-elephants. Kavi became Kavita again, dark eyes aswirl with a new kind of turmoil.

And Cokas was reunited with his ancestors.

By the time the sky brightened, Cokas was gone. His soul was up there among the rain clouds: a spirit, dangerous and unpredictable and everlastingly travelling on the wind. Cokas had joined the great Horde of the Dead.

They found the cart, buried beyond its wheels, where they had abandoned it to go and quell the elephants. Still aboard were the sleeping mats and fleeces, the sodden family kibitki. But of Cokas there was not a trace. It was as if the rain had sluiced him away, and the mud swallowed him down.

Borte was a widow.

She raged and drank, and threw hot coals at the slave-girl Kavita for letting Cokas die. The neighbours offered little sympathy: a great many men had died in the flood – good men, fit men, men of rank. The neighbours had little pity to spare for Borte, who had lost a sick and helpless husband and might well be better off by it. "God is good," they said flatly, and their faces told her not to argue. "Now you can take a new husband."

If they pitied anyone, it was Rusti. He saw the pitying looks, but mistook them for sympathy over a dead brother.

Borte spat on the ground and said, "That it should come to this! That it should come to the likes of you!"

Creased by grief for his dead brother, Rusti struggled to understand her. "Me?"

"Well?" she barked. "Your brother's dead, isn't he? It falls to you. His duties fall on your shoulders. Aii! For what offence do the ancestors punish me like this?" And her undergarment of spoons and combs and bits and stirrups clonked and clanked, as she shuddered with disgust. "Archh! The shame!" and she spat again, this time full in his face.

Rusti gawked at her, mouth half open, not understanding, not wanting to understand. "What?" he said stupidly, because just at that moment he really wanted to be stupid.

Borte rolled her head and lurched from foot to foot like an elephant in distress: "Archh! And must I be *married* to such a fool?"

Chapter Five

Hate

No days were given over to preparations. Rations were low: no time to squander food on a wedding feast. A few words, a few rites, and Rusti and Borte would be man and wife. Well, boy and wife.

The marriage took place under a full moon as round as a battle shield. The moonbeams came down white as blades. Rusti waited for his bride in the rain, sitting astride his horse, watching the beast's ears swivel uneasily, its breath turn to steam. From here and there in the darkness came the wailing of mourners keening over the death of child or parent, wife or husband in the floods.

But the neighbours gathered round, as they might gather round a brawl and cheer on the fighters. They grinned toothless grins at Rusti and shouted dirty jokes he did not understand, hacking up phlegmy coughs and cheers that sounded like jeering. They saw it as a chance to drown their troubles. After the ceremony, they would drink every drop of koumis, eat every morsel of food left in Cokas's tent, then go, without leaving any presents, blaming the mud and bad luck.

Rusti lifted himself clear of the saddle to let the rainwater empty out from under him. The bride was so long in coming that even the snorts of laughter had fallen silent by the time the gossips fetched her out of the kibitki. She looked like a sacrificial beast being led to the slaughter. Her women friends yodelled and warbled wedding chants, but the struggle had worn them out. It had taken all their energy to persuade Borte to let down her hair and to prise her out of her rattling underwear of loot.

"Someone will steal it," she greeted her bridegroom, hissing the words in his face. "If it gets stolen, it's your fault." And her face was livid with rage and cosmetics. Her pony bit into the flank of Rusti's mount whose feet were too deeply sunk in mud to kick back.

The ancestors were summoned to witness the marriage.

"My father would never have let this happen to me," said Borte under her breath.

The mention of fathers brought childish tears to Rusti's eyes. He liked what he remembered of his own father, a powerful, big man who might have fathered *other* sons for Borte to marry, if he had not died: sons Borte would have preferred: sons more like Cokas. Marriages are terrible for making you miss people who ought to be there and are not. That night, Rusti even missed his mother – and she had been dead so long he did not even remember her.

A drink of koumis was served to bride and groom in a single cup. Borte drank first then thrust the cup so sharply at Rusti that its contents slopped into his hair.

The maulana mumbled a prayer and invited them to join hands. Rusti reached out to do as he was told, but Borte had clenched her two hands into a single fist, shut so tight that her knuckles felt huge and glossy. She seemed to be forbidding her hands from giving anything at all to Rusti. Their knees banged together. The ponies began to circle each other, spooked by the mood of their riders.

Just then, Emir Tamburlaine, borne on his litter, passed by on one of his nightly tours of inspection. Noticing the little knot of spectators, he ordered his bearers towards it. So, like a man riding a magic carpet, he floated miraculously into Rusti's line of vision. For the first time in weeks, the Emir's lined, leathery face broke into a smile. "A marriage!" he said. "My elephant boy is marrying!"

The crowd (for all it was obliged to fall respectfully to its knees in the mud) was overjoyed. The evening was suddenly lucky. The bridegroom soared in their estimation: a personal favourite of the Gungal Emir! The Lord of the Fortunate Conjunction had turned the light of his face on the happy pair. The women forgot their weariness and began to sing.

"Many sons to you," mumbled the Emir and floated on his way, but the guests (they were guests now, not just spectators) took up the blessing.

"Many sons to you, elephant boy!"

Rusti coloured with delight. Now perhaps Borte would think better of him too and remember that he was, after all, a warrior of the Horde.

"Live long Rusti, and have many sons!" chanted the neighbours.

Borte leaned towards him across the gap between the two ponies and whispered to him in a voice too low for anyone else to hear:

"Die young, like a dog in a ditch…*tajik*."

* * *

Bad luck was indeed ruling the heavens: it was a terrible season among Tamburlaine's nomadic army. After the floods came disease. The Royal Chronicler Shidurghu wrote of the mud, wrote of the sickness, wrote of the setbacks that so unfairly afflicted the glorious Gungal Emir.

Nobody wrote about Rusti's sufferings. Under the great rolling wheels of History, the story of one young boy is easily pressed into the mud. Besides, there must be worse things than being married to a shrewish wife who hates you.

"But *why* she hate you?" asked Kavi, as they led the elephants down to a river to wash them.

"She calls me a tajik," said Rusti. The injustice of it baffled him. Maybe Borte thought of the elephants as tajiks, and that he had taken on their "tajik-ness" in the same way that he had taken on their smell. Phoolenda the bull-elephant sank onto his side in the water, and Rusti began scrubbing extra hard at his wrinkled grey skin. "Maybe it is just the worst bad word she knows," he said miserably. "Maybe she just thinks I'm unlucky."

"That cannot be," said Kavi. "Crooked Pig Emir like you. You do not die in flood. You do not die in sickness. You have luck big like elephant."

Rusti wondered if his "luck" was too big, and that was why it did not fit inside the family dwelling. He certainly did not feel lucky whenever he had to go home to his bride. "Maybe I'm too young?" Yes, perhaps that was it. Perhaps Borte thought that his twelve years made her, at twenty-seven, look foolish and old. "Or maybe she blames me for being alive when Cokas isn't. The ancestors should have taken me instead. I'm not handsome like Cokas."

Kavi gave a snort of laughter that Cokas should be called "handsome", with his saddlebag cheeks and mean, puffy eyes.

"It's true, I look nothing like him. I'm never going to be big like Cokas was. I never seem to grow." A familiar, wistful regret swept through Rusti, and he stood looking at his slender little shadow lying along the riverbank.

"But she hate you *before*. You say. She hate you always. Before Cokas die."

And it was true. Long before Rusti had given up trying to grow tall and handsome and clever, Borte had loathed him. "Maybe she knows about *you*, then."

But even as he said it he knew it could not be true. Borte would have killed Kavi on the spot if she had realized her slave-girl was a boy in disguise: an enemy in the camp.

"You kill her, yes? You kill her when she sleep!" suggested Kavi enthusiastically.

Rusti laughed. These days Kavi often came out with remarks like that: his thoughts circled the idea of murder, round and round, like flies buzzing round raw meat. And it was funny to hear such bloodthirsty words coming out of this small willowy person in a dress. Besides, the idea of Rusti murdering Borte was like a mosquito plotting to stab an elephant to death. So Rusti laughed and gave Kavi a friendly kind of push.

Inside Kavi's head there was no laughing: none at all. Kavi remembered the massacre of the prisoners. Kavi remembered the fall of Delhi. Kavi remembered the carcasses of the dead elephants lying like so many bloodstained boulders on the plain. He also remembered how easily these same all-conquering Mongols had been killed themselves by a few drops of rain.

Now, each time the Horde passed through a gorge, Kavi found himself trying to conjure landslides. When they were fording a river, he pictured dangerous currents and hidden depths snatching them under and drowning them. When the Horde entered forests, he tried, by force of will, to make a single tree fall, fetching down another and another until the whole forest would come crashing down and bury the Mongols under trunks and branches. When they camped around a lake, Kavi tried to conjure crocodiles by the thousand, with jaws the length of a man and an appetite for flesh.

Forced to play the gentle, harmless girl on the outside, he made up for it on the inside, with thoughts of blood and slaughter… And he did not need Rusti's permission to wish Borte dead; he already prayed for it night and morning.

It was harder to go on hating Rusti. Rusti would persist in being *friendly*! Kavi would have liked to keep things simple. He would have liked just to hate every Mongol alive, with all his might and main. Why, he only had to catch sight of his own girl's clothing, or smell the scent of the almond oil on his hair, to fan the embers of his hate. The Crooked Pig Tamburlaine had reduced him to this – robbed him of family and freedom and dignity and turned him into something ridiculous. So Kavi spent a lot of time thinking about dire revenge. He imagined putting a poisonous snake into Borte's bed. He imagined setting light to the crimson robes or golden brocaded white kibitki of that crippled butcher Tamburlaine. He imagined slicing the heads off all the officers of the Royal Court.

I might just let Rusti live, "Kavita" told himself each night as he combed scented oil into his long, luxuriant hair. *If he gets down on his knees and begs.*

Chapter Six

Found Out

Bath time for the elephants would have been a happy time, no matter what. The huge animals relished it so much that they would speed up at the very sight of a river, shortening their stride into a comical, mincing trot, then flopping into the water like a collapsing riverbank. They would guzzle up gallons, then begin splashing and cavorting about, without a thought for their dignified status as Royal Elephants of the Gungal Emir. Rusti and Kavi got soaked, so they left their clothes on the bank, out of harm's way. But no one saw the elephants cavorting, because no one else came near. The Horde kept up its superstitious fear of the beasts. Rhinoceroses look stupid. Goats look edible. Rats can be clubbed to death with a mallet. But elephants, with their huge, domed foreheads, terrifying tusks and nimble feet, look clever as well as fearsome. Rusti and the Mighty Tamburlaine himself were probably the only two Mongols in the entire Horde who were glad to have the elephants along.

The more time Rusti spent with them, the fonder he grew of Mumu and the rest. Each had a different personality. There was Gajanan with his rumbling guts; Gulab with her fussing; nervy little Alpa, who always kept hold of another elephant's tail for fear of being left behind. There was Damini who picked up his feet as if he was walking on nettles. One was called Gaurang, because of the paleness of his hide, and one, Mahamati, because she had the biggest brain box of all. And there was Phoolenda whose youthful dung was always a different colour from that of the older elephants. Phoolenda would spend a lot of time studying the dung of the older elephants, warming one foot at a time over it, longing (presumably) to match its splendour. Gajanan's name meant that he looked like an elephant.

"What else would he look like?" asked Rusti, when he heard this.

"I not name him," said Kavi with a shrug.

In shallow water the elephants would lie luxuriantly, legs cocked up like dogs wanting their bellies scratched with the boys' twig brooms. In deep water they would almost dance, geysers of silver water bursting into the sky from their upraised trunks. Yes, bath time was best of all. Best of all, because there was no chance of Borte coming anywhere near, no risk of discovery for Kavi. The two boys played and laughed and scrubbed and stood in bare feet on living, breathing stepping stones in the river, surrounded by the giggles of running water. And if they fell in, the sun dried them.

At bath time, Rusti forgot that his wife called him a tajik and spat at him. Sometimes Kavi even put aside his own rage – like the dress he hung from a tree on the riverbank so as to play stark naked. And they vied to see who could jump from Deepti's shining spine onto Elephant-Face Gajanan, and back again without falling in. Then Kavi challenged Rusti to mortal combat and they tried to push each other off their slippery grey islands with the twig brooms. Rusti lost, and as he heaved himself out of the water again onto Damini's rump, he happened to glance over at the bank. That was when he saw the man in the shadow of the trees. Watching. They were being watched.

An old man was standing, one hand looped around the gauzy cotton of Kavita's dress.

A local peasant, thinking to steal it. That would be all right: Rusti could chase after him and take it back. An elderly thief. That would be all right.

But the old man's clothes were not local. They were Mongol.

A poor old Mongol, then, who had outlived his warrior days and his teeth, and was living on charity: that would be all right. For a few coins, or a plate of stew, he might be persuaded to keep quiet about what he had seen.

But the old man's clothes were not poor. He was dressed in the finest of robes. This was a man of wealth and rank. Worse on worse: when the sun went behind a cloud and the dazzle died off the water, Rusti could see the man more clearly – well enough to recognize him. It was Shidurghu the Chronicler, writer-down of History, a minister who every day sat at the feet of the Gungal Emir. For fully fifty heartbeats Rusti stood still, looking back at the man, waiting.

Terror bit into his guts like a river crocodile. He wanted to tell Kavi: *We've been seen! We've been found out!* But what was the point? Why share the fear? He looked up at his friend – skin gleaming, long black hair plastered to his shoulders, whirling his broom over his head and whooping with triumph and glee. Kavi lived his whole life stitched up inside a bag of fear. Let him enjoy a few more minutes free of it. Time enough to suffer when the Chronicler reported what he had seen, when the guards came looking for the "elephant boy" and his "slave-girl", when the death penalty was pronounced.

And when Rusti looked back, the old man was gone. A breeze plucked at the dress in the tree, and set it billowing. It blew this way and that until its thin fabric caught on thorns. But beyond it, there was no one.

"What?" said Kavi, following his gaze.

"Oh," said Rusti. "Nothing." Kavi would find out soon enough. Surely, within the day justice would fall on them both like an axe. Rusti had seen men executed – their backs broken over a rock, a club blow to the head; heads bowling away from the axe. Knowing he was going to be sick, he slid down from Deepti's back and went ashore. Rivers should never be polluted. Being a nomad, Rusti had known that all his life.

He thought of running away. But Rusti was a herd animal, like a sheep or a horse or a cow. He could not imagine being apart from the herd – being one – an individual, rather than one ten-thousandth of the whole. So he helped Kavi pluck the hated dress out of the clutches of the tree and watched him turn himself back into Kavita. *I'm sorry,* he wanted to say. *I am so sorry. We have been found out*. But instead they remounted the elephants and rode back to camp. On the way, they passed the old man, walking. Rusti searched his face for signs of malice or outrage. The pale, filmy eyes met his: blank, inscrutable.

Everything was normal. Borte greeted them as usual: Rusti with a muttered curse, Kavita with a slap to the head. There was no one else. Of course. They were ahead of Shidurghu; he had not yet reached home. Kavita lit a fire using dried dung for fuel, and cooked a dinner: spicy chunks of meat. Borte opened the keg of fermented milk. Three tents away a husband was beating his wife. Somewhere a dog had decided to bark itself hoarse. The meat sat in Rusti's mouth like muddy stones. He could not remember how to swallow. He drank some koumis to wash it down. Koumis, sour and curded. It turned his stomach. This evening was no different. It swilled around in his stomach like seawater in the bilges of a ship. But he drank more, in the hope it would stop him from thinking. Still no one came.

Borte was surprised by his drinking. She regularly taunted him that he was not man enough to take strong liquor. Seeing how it startled her, Rusti drank some more. Still no one came.

Kavita watched, wide-eyed, out of the shadows. Rusti could see the pale circle of his friend's face, changing shape, like a setting moon: the koumis was melting his eyeballs, making his ears sweat. Funny that Kavita had the job of making this horrible stuff: milking the mares and fermenting their milk. His own religion forbade Kavi to drink strong liquor, so he said. Unmanly religion, obviously. Not that being unmanly mattered as far as Kavita was concerned. The less manly the better, really. At the thought of this, Rusti gave a snort of laughter that brought koumis spluttering down his nose. Still no one came to drag him away for harbouring a tajik boy.

Maybe the old Chronicler was blind and had seen nothing? Yes, that must be it! Or maybe he was so old that his memory failed, and he forgot the thing before he even got back to his tent? So no one would come, after all! Rusti was not found out. No one would hack Kavi limb from limb. No one would drag Rusti to death behind a galloping horse.

Not that they would *ever* be so careless again. He

would tell Kavi tomorrow, "You must be Kavita from now on, every moment of the day and night."

The koumis in his stomach turned to something hard and toxic. When he tried to get up and go outside, he was too drunk to stand. A tiny blacksmith inside his head began to beat out pain – to forge pain and nail it in a horseshoe shape round the back of Rusti's skull. He fell against his wife and was very, very sick.

He expected her to hit him, to scream and rage and bewail the miserable fate that had saddled her with such a husband. But in that instant Borte's hatred of him turned as cold and solid inside her as rancid koumis. "You filthy tajik," she said. "Sleep light. One night, I'll kill you where you lie!"

Then there was a massive *THWACK* of wood against hide, and the air filled up with choking dust. Someone had struck the wall of the tent, using the shaft of a spear. Now the spear's end jerked in at the door and lifted the heavy flap aside. "The elephant boy must come," barked the Royal Guard. "Elephant boy to the Royal Compound."

* * *

Outside, the guard rapped the spear against Rusti's hand. He looked down stupidly at his reddened knuckles, before realizing that he was meant to take hold. Then the guard set off at a loping run, and Rusti, towed along behind, had to run his fastest to keep up. In this way, presumably, the guard did not have to demean himself by either touching or speaking to the boy he had been sent to fetch.

Weaving in and out of tents, jumping animal tethers and guy ropes, avoiding small children and treading on the occasional drunk, they ran for at least two miles, through the straggling immensity of the Horde, to where a spinney of glistening banners and pennons flapped against a pink sunset.

There was the Gungal Emir's travelling palace – a small hill of spotted hides, carpets, furs and tapestries, tasselled with horse tails. Gathered around it, and looking like men crouched in prayer, were the tents of his sons, a wife or two, his chief ministers and generals. The spear was wrenched out of Rusti's hand, and the Royal Guard, without a word or a blow, ran on his way, leaving Rusti standing at the door of a magnificent kibitki. In that moment, a melting fear went through Rusti that made his legs sag and his hands cramp shut to catch their own sweat.

Not one but four lamps were burning within the tent, lighting up an interior large enough for a family of twelve. And yet only one man slept between the hanging panels of brocade and the fleece rugs. There was spindle-legged furniture from countries a year's ride to the west. This was the tent of Shidurghu, the Royal Chronicler, writer-down of History for the Lord of the Fortunate Conjunction.

"Step forward, Rusti," said Shidurghu, his face a livid yellow in the light from the lamps. And as Rusti stumbled over the threshold, Shidurghu opened a drawer and took out a small sharp knife. "Come here, boy. I have to question you."

Chapter Seven

Words and Pictures

On the table in front of the old man lay a pile of parchments, pinned down at each corner with carved lumps of polished wood.

"Elephants," he said, turning on Rusti a face as unreadable as the letters written in front of him.

"Yes," said Rusti stupidly.

"Today I went to look."

"Yes," said Rusti. And then, "Yes, Your Honour."

"Come close. I need your eyes," and Shidurghu picked up a small knife.

Rusti clapped both hands over his eye sockets and imagined blindness. It was not a punishment he had been expecting. His legs shook uncontrollably.

"You refuse to look at my elephants?"

Rusti parted his hands. Was this, then, the last sight he would see? An old man, mildly put out, sharpening the quill of a feather to a point?

Suddenly Shidurghu slapped the back of one hand against the papers on his desk. "Pigs! I draw elephants and I have pigs!" Then, leaning on one elbow, the Chronicler rested his head on one hand and regarded the parchment in front of him, lips pushed out in a pout of dissatisfaction.

Rusti looked. He could see nothing at first because of the tears of fright in his eyes, but blinking them furiously away he finally made out pictures at the edge of the pages, like patterns bordering a carpet. The pigs to which the old man referred were chalked on a piece of slate. Over and over again. Long-nosed pigs.

"It's the legs," Rusti said. "They bend the other way. Not like horses. Like…like… Well. Like elephants, Your Honour."

"Ah!" Wiping the slate with one sleeve (Borte would have killed Rusti for letting a single grain of chalk touch such a sleeve!) Shidurghu chalked a new sketch.

"And the eye is lower? The head bigger?" suggested Rusti. And when he could not describe what was wrong with the tusks, he drew it himself:

the Chronicler put the chalk into his hand. Rusti had scratched many pictures of elephants in the dusty ground. But never had he seen the like of the elephants that flowed from Shidurghu's quill pen after that. The Chronicler made quick small strokes that fetched a scratchy whisper from the parchment. And like twigs drifting together in a moving river, the sketch somehow built up. They created the likeness of an elephant. It was still something long in the legs and short in the trunk, but it was definitely an elephant. Unmistakably an elephant. Rusti marvelled as he watched: a whole caravan of elephants standing about at the edge of a forest of writing.

"When the ink is dry I shall add more colours," said Shidurghu. "Red. Gold. Small houses on their backs, as at Delhi." And Rusti remembered with a jolt the howdahs strapped to the elephants' backs on the day he first saw them. After the battle the elephants of Delhi had been reduced to bare-backed beasts, maimed and scarred. Rusti had forgotten, until now, those miniature palaces of crimson and gold that had housed flamethrowers, spear wielders and mahouts.

The old man's fingers were long and pale, the backs of his hands mapped with big purple veins. Not Mongol hands. A foreigner.

"What does it say?" asked Rusti, without knowing he had been going to speak at all.

"I write of the Great Conquest of Delhi, when the Mighty Emir, Glory of the World, captured the City of Gems and put to flight the powers of obstinacy and error. I write so that the air may be filled with his praise as the sky is filled with birds at sunset." (He used such words! Rusti had never exactly thought of the Great Emir as "a snowy swan upon a lake of blood" or "the shining face of genius and might", but of course if the Chronicler said he was, in that matter-of-fact voice, then it must be true.) Shidurghu drew an elephant upside down at the foot of the page, its trunk severed from its body, but its howdah still in place and its legs straight up in the air as if it were floating downriver rather than rolling over in death onto its knobbly spine. Sprinkling sand over the wet ink, he picked up the page and shook off the surplus. Underneath lay another sheet strewn with more horizontal figures. Men. Women. Children. It was a picture of the massacre of prisoners. "Behold the ungrateful rebels who defied the will of Our Mighty Emir, Lord of the Fortunate Conjunction and Bringer of Mercy, and had to be punished." His voice was as flat as the battlefield.

Rusti's mind tried to swerve round the memories, but they were just too big: one hundred thousand prisoners massacred in the space of days. His nose filled up even now with the smell of it: the blood, the pile of dung he had set alight, to make the Emir think he had done his duty. Another lie. Another betrayal. What a worthless warrior Rusti had proved to be since his first battle! Probably he *deserved* to have his neck broken, or to be dragged to death behind galloping horses.

A further sheet was peeping out from underneath the Great Conquest at Delhi, showing a blue-tinted border. There were the wavy blue lines overtopping the heads of horsemen, overturning carts, weaving their way through huddles of homes. "The floods!" exclaimed Rusti, starting to understand. A marvellous mystery took place inside this tent. Here the past was preserved for ever, on sheets of milk-white parchment. Wait till he told Kavi!

"The floods, yes. When your unfortunate brother Cokas died," said the Chronicler, and looked so intently at Rusti with his pale, foreigner's eyes, that Rusti's fright slithered about inside him like a piece of raw liver. How could Shidurghu, a minister of the Royal Court, *possibly* know anything at all about Cokas, or his obscure twelve-year-old little brother? "I write what I see," said Shidurghu. "I write *everything* I see. Almost. That is my purpose. And I have seen much."

Rusti caught his breath. So here it was. He had not escaped. In a second Shidurghu would say it: that he had seen Rusti and Kavita playing at the river; that he knew Rusti had helped an enemy warrior to escape death, and had hidden him in his tent, disguised as a girl.

Shidurghu was studying him so closely that he seemed about to draw a portrait of Rusti. "I remember when the chariot of our Mighty Emir was drawn by conquered men in place of horses. I remember kings caged and queens manacled in chains...such is the power of War, the might of our Sublime Warrior-King. I remember –" the eyes narrowed for a moment – "I remember another triumph. A victory as glorious as Delhi. Another victor's wreath around the brow of Our Gracious Emir, Pattern of All Excellence. No one should forget these golden achievements of our Magnificent Leader and all that he has done." As he assembled each flat, glittering sentence, he reminded Rusti of a tiler cementing beautiful tiles to a wall, using a dirty rag. "It happened many years ago. Do you wish to see?"

Rusti nodded dumbly. Why would a man of such importance want to show *him* anything at all? He was expecting Shidurghu to fetch out some old parchment from the desk or a trunk. But the old man simply swept the table clear of those precious pages – those priceless, wonderful parchments embellished with mystical swirls of writing. And on a clean piece of parchment he began to draw. Suddenly he was no longer an old man, slow and careful.

Two strokes and there was a hill. Twelve strokes and there was a range of hills with mountains beyond. A clutter of crude huts. A mosque. A wall. A tower – no! A palace. When his hand paused, it was shaking, and although it is not unusual for an old man's hand to shake, it had not been shaking earlier.

"I speak of the glorious victory at Zubihat (may it live long in the memory of the world). Zubihat lies in the province of Sorkh Pash. But when Mighty Tamburlaine added Sorkh Pash to the marvellous Mongol nation, did the foolish sons of Zubihat surrender? No! Did they send shroud and sword and beg for mercy? No! They chose to reject the wise and kindly rule of the Gungal Emir. *Naturally* he had to make an example of them. So he set aside his merciful nature and employed the fist of Might." His voice was sing-song, but at this point his fist shot out and punched a saddle hanging from the roof. The pen clenched in his fist broke and crumpled.

Ow, thought Rusti, but Shidurghu did not seem to notice any pain. Throwing aside the broken quill, he sharpened another to a point and began drawing again. A tower?

"A tower without doors," said the Chronicler. *Scritch-scratch* and he had created a plain beyond the tower – *scritch-scratch* – and on it a jumble of boots, shields, helmets, limbs, heads and horses upside down. A few inky ticks, and crows were circling overhead.

Just as they had twelve years before.

There were odd shapes sticking out from the sides of the tower, like buds blossoming on a twig. Rusti could not make out what they were supposed to be. Shidurghu gave a shrill, unexpected bleat. "Defy the Lord of the Fortunate Conjunction? Such things cannot be allowed to happen! Surely the sky would fall. Surely the rivers would freeze! Surely the sea would run dry! Defy Tamburlaine the Great? Ambassadors come to visit this demi-god, from kingdoms the world over, to heap on him gifts and flattery and treaties and purses of money. And does

Zubihat dare to cross him? Then it must be taught a lesson! And so, after the battle of Zubihat is won, a tower is built. And into it are put all the women, the old men, the children. Babies. Here and there a hole – a piece of shoddy building – so that hands reach out. And voices, of course."

Rusti could not take his eyes off the picture of that tower. Not buds blossoming, then. Hands. Dozens and dozens of hands. A townful of women and children walled up inside a tower, thrusting out their hands through holes in the brickwork. Rusti could smell the perfumed oil on their hair.

"Voices, of course. Calling out," said the old man. His own voice had become a peculiar, one-note whisper, and his mouth was rucked out of shape. "I find these events strange. But then I am a foreigner. To a Mongol hero there is no dishonour in stealing from the dying, in tormenting the helpless, in killing women and children. Daily I record such acts of... *bravery* in my Chronicles. One day all the world may read what I have written, and marvel at the deeds of Mighty Tamburlaine... But I was speaking of the baby, wasn't I?" Shidurghu's voice became sing-song and breezy once again.

"Baby?" whispered Rusti. "No. What baby?"

Shidurghu picked up a chess piece from the corner of a nearby chessboard – a black turret-piece – and set it down on the parchment. It was as if the tower had taken on solid form once more:

"There is a boy – no older than yourself – riding in the company of his father, Baliq."

"Oh! That was my father's name," said Rusti, amused by the coincidence, then suffered a pang of fear: did that count as naming the Dead, he wondered? Shidurghu did not allow it to interrupt his story.

"Baliq, yes. The boy's name is Cokas."

"Cokas?" said Rusti, but he was in the middle of swallowing, and no noise came out. Not an uncommon name, and yet... Rusti could not help now picturing his brother, Cokas, as the boy in the story. Cokas alive again, young again. Cokas when he was Rusti's age. Back then, Rusti himself would have been – what? A baby. Just a little baby.

"This is his first siege. Cokas's first battle," Shidurghu was saying. "Naturally he wants proof of his manliness – some loot, some plunder – a present, perhaps for a future bride. His eye is caught by the glint of gold. And so he rides up to the tower, to pluck the bracelet from the wrist reaching through a hole in the wall. It is done in a moment. But the woman has more to give him! Into his hands she thrusts something soft and warm. 'Save my child! My child has done nothing!' And there he is: a boy, holding a baby."

Shidurghu looked at Rusti, as if it was his turn to speak, but Rusti could think of nothing to say. There seemed to be room in his head for only one question, a question too big to squeeze out through his throat: *What baby?*

He tried to speak it, but it wedged in his gullet, like a hand wedged in a gap too narrow; stayed trapped inside him like a child in a tower without doors. Shidurghu went on with his story.

"Warrior-boy Cokas swings the baby by its legs, ready to dash it against the wall, or throw it to the dogs. But his father Baliq stops him – a hand on his sleeve – says they will keep it. Says, 'A man can never have too many sons.' And so warrior boy takes the golden bracelet, and his father takes the baby." Shidurghu sat back in his chair, hands clasped on his stomach, watching Rusti's face intently. "What do you say, boy? Was the father wise to take this baby? Was he wise to call it a son? Was he wise to foist this small creature on his family? Was he wise to make his son vow to treat it like a brother? The thing was a *tajik*, after all. Dangerous. Might it not carry inside it the failings of a *tajik*? Pity? Mercy? Gentleness?" The old man spat after each word, though Rusti noticed he was not very good at spitting and thought perhaps he did not do it very often.

A rime of sweat had formed on Rusti's top lip, like the beginning of a moustache. (When had it arrived? He could not tell.) One single word was filling his head to bursting. One word. What did it look like? This wise man knew words. He could draw their portraits out of loops and lines and pen strokes.

"Honoured Shidurghu," said Rusti. "Please write a word for me."

For the first time, the Chronicler was startled. His heavy lids lifted for the briefest moment. "What word, boy? Your name? There. RUSTI. A good Mongol name. Given you, like any name, when you had no other."

Rusti looked at his name on the parchment and shook his head. It was not the right word, and anyway he could not see it. (When had he started to cry? He could not tell.) Still the right word kept jabbing his brain with its sharp hooks and loops.

"Shall I teach you how to write it yourself?" said Shidurghu, reaching out the quill towards Rusti. A single drop of ink welled up at its tip and dropped onto the precious carpet. Rusti closed his hands into fists and stepped backwards. Write a word? The very idea was preposterous. Almost as preposterous as the idea that he, Rusti, could be…could ever have been… could possibly be…

"Not 'Rusti'. My wife calls me by another name," he blurted, and Shidurghu dipped his quill into the ink again. "Will you write down that name for me, honoured Shidurghu?"

And obligingly – *scritch-scratch* – the old man wrote what Rusti told him – wrote it, in his mysterious, silent, inky, coded, curlicue letters:

TAJIK.

Chapter Eight

Bad Dreams

He did not tell Kavi – not even Kavita (although Kavita would have understood about being one thing on the outside and another on the inside). Nor did he tell Borte that he understood now why she called him "tajik".

Shidurghu gave him the parchment as a gift, and Rusti took it home with him. He wanted to look and to look and to look until his eyes wore out the ink and he could see inside that inky cylinder of bricks, that tower: until he could see the women shut up inside.

Borte demanded to see what he had brought back from his meeting with the Royal Chronicler – "What is it? Give it here!"– and snatched the page out of his hands. But she made no sense of the sketchy lines;

mistook the tower and its waving hands, for a tree in blossom. "Why did the Chronicler send for you?" she asked accusingly.

"He was drawing elephants. I showed him how elephants fold their legs."

"Elephants. Elephants," snarled Borte, unable to think of an appropriate insult. He thought she might tear the parchment into pieces or burn it during one of her rages, so he slid it under his bedroll, and when it came to striking camp and packing away their belongings, he carried it inside his clothing. A woman inside a tower, inside a roll of parchment, inside his shirt.

Inside his head.

Rusti looked at it in secret: at the warriors lying dead on the battlefield. *One of those must be the baby's father,* he decided. *That helmet, there. That shield. They were his. The father's. My...*

But however hard he studied the inky picture, it would not show him the women inside the tower. Only his dreams took him there.

He began to have dreams every single night – terrible, shifting dreams; lightless, sweating dreams in which he was sealed up in a tiny space, crushed and barged by soft dark shapes he could not see. Oh, and he did *try to see*. In his dreams, he peered through the darkness until his eyeballs were dry from trying. And he tried to scrabble through the wall that penned him in, but his hands were soft as candle wax. He tried to force a way out, pushing with all his might against the bricks. Once he dreamed of a golden bracelet and knew that if he could just make himself small enough to squeeze through its tiny circle then he would be free! But he was too hulking big – big like Cokas, big like Borte, big like a Mongol pony, big like an elephant…

Rusti's dreams were full of noise and terror, his ears full of shrieking and wailing and metal scraping stone. And he woke with his ears full of saltwater, where his own tears had run down as he slept and filled the hollows.

Then he hated himself, because only tajiks cry.

"Tell me about Delhi," he said to Kavi the next time they were scrubbing clean the elephants. He could remember how, after the fall of Delhi, Kavi had been eaten up with homesickness.

But how could Kavi, with his few learned Mongol words, even begin to describe to Rusti the sunlit courtyards of his home city, the orange groves, the festivals, the markets, the sunsets, the gardens? How could he conjure up the watermelon sellers or the workshops at the end of his lane where he had watched carpenters build the howdahs to be strapped to elephants' backs? Reddled leather straps drying in the sunshine. Besides, these days all Kavi remembered was the slaughter, the fire, the humiliation of defeat.

Rusti wanted to know how it felt to live in a city all year round, to plant crops and see them grow, to harvest them and eat them under the same rag of sky. He wanted to know. He wanted to know how it felt to be a tajik. But his friend could not tell him.

And Kavi was having dreams of his own.

Kavi dreamed every night that he was standing near the Gungal Emir. Sometimes, on cold nights, the dream placed them on a cliff top, and Kavi would step up and put his hands against the Crooked Pig's crooked back and try to push him over the edge, to watch him falling, falling. But his feeble pushes only dab-dab-dabbed against the quilted robe.

And sometimes, on stuffy nights, Kavi dreamed he was in a dark tent, with barely light enough to see by, but knowing that the dark shape in front of him was the Crooked Pig. Then Kavi's hands would close around a brass candlestick or a tent pole or a cooking pot, and he would go to batter and bludgeon the life out of the detested old butcher.

But he could never hit hard enough; his arms were not strong enough! *Pat, pat, pat* his blows would fall, like snow on a sheep, and he would wake grunting with effort, sweating with frustration, sobbing with unspent hatred.

"I kill Gungal Rat. One day," said Kavita to Rusti, the next time they were scrubbing clean the elephants. "One day I rip heart." Then he looked up and smiled: gentle, soft-spoken, doe-eyed Kavita, with his long, glossy hair and his soul of dry steel. And Rusti laughed, of course...because that is what you do, isn't it, when someone is talking nonsense?

Chapter Nine

Turret

The next week, Rusti was summoned again to the Chronicler's kibitki. His head teemed with unanswered questions – *Was it me? Was that baby really and truly me?* – but Shidurghu did not wish to talk. He wished simply to play chess. That week, the next week, and every week thereafter.

The guards in the Royal Encampment wondered at it at first – supposed the elephant boy must have a genius for chess as well as elephants. But they grew used to the sight of him plodding towards them on his disreputable pony, dismounting outside the Chronicler's white tent flap, taking off his muddy boots. Soon the sight was so familiar that they lost interest, ceased even to talk about him behind his back.

Rusti *never* grew used to the sight of that white tent flap thrown back, the ivory and cedarwood pieces laid out especially for his benefit, the glass of wine poured and waiting. Unlike the guards, he knew he was *not* a genius at chess. Before getting injured, Cokas had played it with him, using home-made chess pieces so crude that it was impossible to tell turret from pawn, even red from black. Rusti had made sure he never won, because Cokas was a bad loser and would have hit him if he had. But there again it had not been all that *difficult* to lose.

Now, here, he was playing against an expert, handling beautifully carved chessmen looted from Tiflis by the Gungal Emir himself. The old man won every game without lending more than half an eye to the board. Losing did not worry Rusti, but it almost broke his heart that Shidurghu did not speak again of Zubihat, or the tower, or the story of the tajik baby.

After each chess game, the old man would show him one letter – one cipher from his strange, secret, inky language – and have Rusti draw it, with a piece of chalk, on a slate: ten, thirty, fifty times, until the boy saw it in his sleep.

The skill of copying letters came to him, but never the skill of words, or of reading. The letters remained decorations, pretty patterns on the vellum. To Shidurghu's gusty annoyance, Rusti simply could not lace them together into words, sound, meaning. Rusti remained a sorcerer's apprentice copying magic spells without knowing what they were for. There was no magic living inside him – he would have felt it if there was.

Perhaps the writing lessons were a punishment for playing chess so badly: Rusti barely bothered to wonder. He was too bewildered as to why he was there – too afraid of the old man and what he knew – too busy hankering after the Story of the Tower. But the subject was never mentioned, and Rusti dared not ask.

Sometimes, Shidurghu asked after Rusti's wife. An odd topic of conversation, but Shidurghu would ask: "How is your wife?" It was something no Mongol would ever have asked his neighbour, and Rusti was at a loss how to answer.

"Rich in loot," he said once, thinking it had a ring to it. Then he heard himself adding: "Underneath she's all spoons and stirrups."

The Chronicler regarded him from under papery, drooping lids. "Her heart also, I think." And Rusti gave a shiver and wondered if the old man knew everything about him, without asking: not just his

Past, but his Present too, and all the things going on inside his head.

Suddenly, after ten weeks – much to his surprise – Rusti started to win at chess. He captured whole battalions of pawns, whole harems of queens. "We should play for more than the honour of winning," said the Chronicler, sitting back while Rusti reset the board.

And that was how Rusti won himself a new pony – a young, fit colt with pretty stripes on its rump and worth a bagful of money. He called the pony Arrow, because the stripes looked like a flight of arrow shafts. A warrior is made or marred by his pony. With Arrow under him, Rusti thought he might at last become a proper warrior rather than a boy – might even *feel* like a proper warrior rather than a boy. He could barely believe his luck.

Borte could barely believe it either. "Did you steal it? You did! You stole it! From the Royal Encampment!" She went at him with both fists. "We'll all be stoned to death! Broken under our own wagon wheels! You magpie! You halfwit! You pilfering little tajik rat!"

Rusti found it difficult to explain. The Chronicler's wine was rather strong and, after two glasses, his brain grew a kind of wool all over it. But since he had *not* stolen Arrow, Borte could hardly complain. The pony was too small for her to ride, so she could not take it for herself: Borte made that her excuse to be furious.

Mounted on Arrow, Rusti began to find the ride to the Royal Encampment less fearful. The old man seemed to like him. The chess was getting easier. (He had already planned his opening gambit for today's game.) Next time he won, he knew what he wanted for a prize. He would ask for the Truth. Once and for all. *Was* he the baby in the story? Who was his true father? Had his mother been set free from the tower, after the conquerors moved on? She had, hadn't she? (For that was what he told himself now, when he woke from his nightmares sweating and breathless.)

The guards outside the white kibitki held the pony's head while Rusti dismounted. (They would never have done *that* a month before!) Rusti wondered if he could bring Kavita along with him one of these days, so that his friend could see the way he was treated, the wonders that lay beyond that dark tent entrance.

"And how is your wife?" Shidurghu asked, as they settled to the second game.

"A credit to her father and a terror to the enemy," said Rusti (who had had time to think up a proper answer). He moved a pawn, releasing the turret-piece in the corner to roam around the board. The first thing he did, in any game, was to free his turret-pieces: he could not relax, somehow, until they had their freedom.

"And how is your servant?"

Rusti knocked over a whole squad of pawns, who rolled onto the floor.

"Kavita?"

"Ah yes," said Shidurghu. "Kavi-ta."

It was not fair. Just when Rusti had forgotten all about the river, the elephants' bath time, here he was, cornered by the Truth.

"I won her. At Delhi," he said, down on his knees, under the table, looking for pawns who had gone into hiding amid the rich patterns of the carpet. "She works. Like slaves should. She helps with the cooking." Rusti plunged on. "And with the elephants."

"Ah! That, boy, is very…*telling*."

Rusti kneeled painfully on a pawn and cursed. Then he banged his head on the underside of the table and fetched a whole host of chessmen blipping down onto him and the floor. "Sorry, sorry, sorry, sorry," he said as each rolled over the edge. "Sorry."

The Chronicler rested the tips of his fingers together and watched Rusti struggle with panic and a headful of lies, none of them big enough to cover the situation. Shidurghu knew about Kavi, and Rusti knew that he knew, and Shidurghu knew that Rusti knew that he knew.

"A good slave is hard to come by," the old man said. "You must keep her safe. Not let her out of your sight."

"Yes. I mean no. Mmmm. Definitely. Yes. A good slave is...like you said."

Shidurghu tapped his fingertips together. "In Samarqand, you will sell her?"

"NO!" Both the place name and the idea caught Rusti off guard. "Why? Are we making for Samarqand?"

"Even the wind turns homeward once in a while," said Shidurghu spreading his palms.

Rusti gathered up all the chess pieces and replaced them on the board. One turret-piece was missing. There was no suggestion of going on with the game. The Chronicler retreated behind closed lids, and Rusti backed awkwardly away – important not to turn his back on such an important man – towards the tent flap and the sunlight. Just as Rusti felt its comforting warmth, Shidurghu spoke again.

"Samarqand. By way of Zubihat," he said.

"Zubihat?"

"So you will be able to see for yourself the mighty works of Tamburlaine." And Shidurghu opened his hand to show the lost turret-piece lying black in his pale palm. Rusti collided with a bridle hanging from the roof, got tangled up in its reins and fetched it down on himself as he struggled to get free. The Chronicler did not even trouble to open his eyes.

Chapter Ten
Warrior Boy

It was true: even the Mongol Horde did not wander about perpetually, aimlessly, like leaves blowing in the wind. The Gungal Emir, Timur the Lame, Lord of the Fortunate Conjunction, was turning towards Samarqand, capital city of his Empire and a place of fabled magnificence. There had to be some spot on the rolling earth where ambassadors could seek audience with him; somewhere to house the chronicles of his daring exploits; somewhere for him to display the works of art he had looted and the presents he had been given by captured cities begging for mercy. There had to be somewhere for his Royal Zoo. Somewhere to sell captives to slavers, or put them to work building endless walls or canals. Somewhere to share out the Empire among his sons.

The Horde headed eagerly for Samarqand as if, like tajiks, they would be happy to get home where they belonged. In fact it was more like a holiday destination, where they would spend a season trading, drinking, bragging, sleeping and getting bored enough to leave again. But after the hardships of this particular campaign, no one was complaining as the Horde flocked northwards towards Samarqand.

Rusti had been there just three times in his short life. He remembered its marvels – squares and streets and brick buildings three storeys high – its mosques and mosaics and the white horses who grazed the peculiarly perfect meadows outside its walls. Best among his memories were the sweet-sellers in the market, their wares set out at eye level (well, it had been a while now), all crawling in flies and a perfume that set his spit running. Worst among his memories was watching his father Baliq die in bed – somewhere indoors – of a rat bite that had turned gangrenous. His last words to Cokas and Borte had been a simple instruction, easily obeyed he supposed: "Keep your oath to me," Baliq had said. But his words to Rusti had left the little boy weeping, powerless to obey. "Take off the ceiling, son. I want to see the stars." Even standing on a chair, the four-year-old Rusti had not been able to perform his father's dying wish. So Rusti had mixed feelings about Samarqand. It spoke to him of failure and ghosts.

And the route home did take them through Zubihat.

Well, they could have skirted by it, of course: taken a different route. But Tamburlaine liked to revisit the scenes of his victories. He liked to make sure that the cities he had captured remembered who had spared their miserable lives, who had broken their pride and rubbed their noses in the dirt. Twelve years was a long time, but Timur had made certain the people of Zubihat would never forget him.

Sitting one night eating his dinner, Rusti heard two old men talking outside the kibitki:

"Two days to Zubihat, by my reckoning."

"…remember that name…forget why."

"The place where we built that tower, yes? For the women, yes? Waste of women, to my way of thinking."

Rusti's ribs closed up tight around his heart so that it did not quite have room to beat. He was about to see the place where he was born. His home. His native valley. Ah but no! That was nonsense! The Chronicler's story had been about some *other* boy, some *other* baby. Unable to breathe, Rusti shouldered his way out of doors, stumbling over Borte, who slapped angrily at his legs. "Clumsy fool! What did I do to deserve such a camel for a husband?"

Outside, he shook his head hard, trying to dislodge all thought of Zubihat from his skull. It only made him dizzy. And the thoughts came back, black as crows. His shadow lay along the ground, slim and slight, jeering at him for ever thinking he might be a Mongol by birth, might one day become a warrior or even a proper man. Rusti kicked dust over his own shadow. "I won't go. They can't make me." He breathed in the comforting smells of the Horde: filth and food and animals. He was the Great Emir's elephant boy. That was all. That was quite enough! Shidurghu had been lying, or mistaken. Or his story had been about some other boy. "I'll go around. I'll take the elephants round another way. Don't need to go there. Nothing to do with me. I won't go."

"Go? Where go?" said Kavita, emerging from the tent with an empty bucket, on his way to fetch water. He flicked his shawl over his head with a gesture unknowingly learned from the female slaves.

"It's a story," said Rusti, and pursed shut his mouth.

"I like story," said Kavita. "Tell."

Rusti looked nervously over his shoulder: the Mongols were a race of spies. "Not here," he said.

So the story was told within the shelter of lazing elephants. In the grey leathery ravine between their knobbly spines, great grey ears fanning away the evening flies, Rusti told Kavi the story of the tower at Zubihat – though of course he did not mention the baby boy. Kavi did not need to know everything. It was just a story, after all.

The closer they came to Zubihat, the more certain Rusti was that he had never been there. Proof! If he had been born in these parts, he would surely recognize the curve of the hills, the stones on the ground, the clouds in the sky.

At night he dreamed he was walking into the place, and that people came running out of their homes, waving and smiling, calling him by name. "Look who's here! Look who it is!" And their dogs wanted to lick him, and the women wanted to cook him supper, but he kept trying to point to Kavi somewhere behind him, and to say, "No, not me. It's him. He's the tajik!

Not me, him!" When he woke, he told himself there was no truth in dreams.

He was right.

There *were* no people in Zubihat.

Oh, there were a few settlements nearby. Even some of the houses they passed were built of stone carried away from the demolished town. But Zubihat itself had not been rebuilt after its defeat at the hands of Tamburlaine. It had been abandoned: a place of ghosts; a place poisoned by memories, as a waterhole can be poisoned by the body of a dead dog. The air was dank with sorrow, and people do not choose to raise their children where the air is bad.

As Tamburlaine's elephants passed by the ruins, Mahamati twitched her ears and stepped anxiously from foot to foot: her rider was sitting so rigid in the crease of her neck, that she could not understand what the boy wanted of her. Her trunk reached back and kissed his arm, his kneecaps, questioning. But Rusti simply sat and looked around him. Kavita sat alongside, riding Gaurang whose pale hide made her look ashen with fear or sorrow. It is frightening, after all, to ride across the pages of a story, especially a true one.

* * *

Within sight of the tower, they pitched camp, eating supper under a rosy evening sky. The old men settled to telling stories of their heroism during the fall of Zubihat. There was a festive mood; laughter flittered overhead amid the bats. Everything made for laughter among the veteran warriors and their bloodthirsty children: the cowardice of the citizens of Zubihat, the weakness of the defending soldiers, the way the tajiks had pleaded for their lives…

How is that funny? thought Rusti. But looking across the campfire at his wife, he saw her laughing with all the rest. Once, her eyes turned in his direction, and her expression changed to loathing. Was she comparing him with his dead brother Cokas? Or was she recalling how, twelve years before, Cokas and his father had helped to build that tower yonder, and had taken away with them a couple of souvenirs: a gold bracelet and a baby boy? All he had to do was ask her – call out to her now through the smoke of the bonfire; whisper the question in her ear before they went to sleep. *"That tower over there: is that why you call me a tajik? Is that where I came from?"* But the question stuck in his throat. It seemed to have been walled up inside him, and could not break out.

He needed to know!

Unable to eat, unable to sleep, Rusti went looking for the Royal Chronicler, Shidurghu – rode Arrow recklessly fast, towards the fluttering bannerettes of the Royal Encampment. He would ask the man straight out: was it true? But the tent of the Royal Chronicler was not pitched alongside the others of the Royal Court. Like a white chess piece, it had been removed from the board.

The guards waved Rusti away: no chess-playing boys needed this evening: Shidurghu had gone upcountry with the Gungal Emir, to act as his interpreter. After all: this was his native district, they said. The Chronicler was a Zubihat man himself.

"Of course. I forgot," said Rusti as if he had known all along. He did not let his face register any of the things hammering at his heart.

Back by the campfire, Borte had begun to dance, flirting with a neighbour whose wife had died in childbirth that day; vowing to put a smile back on his face... Rusti could see the shape of her big body, flabby and smooth through the cloth of her robe. She was clearly not wearing her chain mail of loot.

Ducking inside the family tent, Rusti began to search. There was no lamp, and it was very dark. Something moved in the shadows, and he reared up guiltily from his hands and knees. Only Kavita.

"Where is it?" Rusti hissed. "She's not wearing it. Help me find her loot! I have to find it!"

With silent footfall, Kavita crossed the rug, unlaced a bedroll and unrolled it, loosing its sour, sweaty smell. There was a tinkling of metal, as Borte's spoils of war spilled out of it. Rusti had never before examined his wife's booty, never even touched any of the bridle-rings and belt buckles, the helmet spikes, or strings of foreign coins.

"What you look?" asked Kavi.

"A bracelet. A golden bracelet!" Of course, Cokas might have kept the bracelet himself – not given it to his wife when they married. Or Borte might have sold it when times were hard. Anyway, there *was* no golden bracelet, because the whole thing had happened to someone else, hadn't it? Or because Shidurghu was lying and the whole thing had never happened at all!

Kavi leaned across and picked up a glittering O from among the other dross; picked it up and handed it to Rusti without a word. His dark, scratched fingers were so slender they could almost have belonged to a woman: a woman reaching through a hole in rough brickwork, to buy mercy with a golden bracelet.

Of course the world has produced a great many golden bracelets. This one might have come from anywhere – from Tiflis or Baghdad. But to Rusti it was proof – absolute proof – of Shidurghu's story. For a moment he held the warm metal against his cheek. And from that moment he believed.

"Will you come back here with me?" he urged in a whisper. "After the rest move on? Will you come back here with me?"

In the darkness of the tent, nothing showed but the liquid glimmer of Kavi's big, dark eyes. Then his head tilted slightly to one side and he pushed his long hair clear of his ears to listen.

"Someone come," he said.

Pure terror went through Rusti, thinking it was Borte returning to the tent. He pushed the bracelet inside his clothes, bundled the loot clumsily back into the mattress and rolled it up. What if she caught him meddling with her warrior hoard? She would break his neck – or take a cleaver to him.

But Kavi had picked up a sound much farther off – beyond the usual rowdy clamour of drunkenness, quarrels and children. He rested the flat of his hand on the floor, feeling vibrations. "Horses," he said. "Big many horses."

And all of a sudden, the evening noises of eating, drinking and brawling changed, and the Horde gave a shout, as with one voice. The encampment was under attack…

Women screamed their children's names. Drinkers cursed. Kibitkis slumped flat with a noise like collapsing camels. Dogs barked. Ponies snorted and whinnied. Kavi looked around for somewhere to hide. With a soft thud, something struck the roof above his head, and an arrowhead pierced the felt and hide, and came sliding through for most of its length. It did not matter that it had lost its momentum, for it came fletched with fire. At once, the burning arrow began to char the fabric of the roof. Quickly Kavi pulled it right through the kibitki wall and plunged it in the cooking pot.

Squirming outside, Rusti was blinded by the last, low rays of the sun, billowing smoke and divots of mud thrown up by a passing rider. His neighbour's pony lay dying, with an arrow in its throat. His thieving neighbour was kneeling to free Rusti's pony of its hobble. It took five heartbeats. Rusti waited until the fifth, then leaped onto Arrow's back and took off at a gallop, toppling the neighbour onto his face in the mud.

There were a million sights to take in, and any one might mean the difference between life and death. *Attack out of the sunset. Element of surprise. Who? Few helmets. No banners. Targes – just like his own little shield. What shield?* Rusti turned his pony in a circle so tight that its nose touched its rump, and galloped back to the kibitki.

"Kavi! Weapons! Sword! Shield!" Three heartbeats. Four. The weapons flew out of the doorway of the kibitki, thrown as hard as Kavita's puny arms would allow. Rusti had to lean right down to the ground to pick them up. The targe rolled along on its rim and Rusti had to snatch it up at the gallop. *Felt better for succeeding. Felt better for the shape of a sword hilt in his hand, the weight of leather on his arm. Must see everything. Notice everything. Life depends on it. Cavalry streaming down from the Royal Encampment. Defenders. Must tell them apart. How? Poor light. Arrows from where? Horizontal? Or out of the sky? Axes and scimitars. A few halberds. A sickle? Peasants, then. Blacksmith's wagon, on fire. Riderless camel, mad with panic.* Rusti had the impression that he was watching the battle through a long dark tunnel – that he was not somehow a part of it. Strange how the mind becomes detached...

Strange altogether. A minute before, he had been

scared – terrified at the thought of Borte catching him. Now they were under attack, and he was hardly scared at all; hardly of anything. *Must see everything, notice everything. Three children hand-in-hand, eyes shut, as if told not to look. Pail of milk knocked over.*

The runaway camel tripped on a guy rope and crashed down, one of the bristly lumps on its head brushing Rusti's legs. "Where are the elephants?" he said aloud, and the camel's teeth burst ajar as if it was about to gasp an answer. The blacksmith ran by with his clothes on fire. The defending cavalry swept past in a blur and collided with the attackers, like waves breaking against rocks. Two ponies fell. Arrow stepped on something soft and broke her stride so sharply that Rusti shot forward and bruised himself on the sharp base of her neck.

"Blind rats!" yelled a familiar voice. It was Borte, and for a moment Rusti assumed she was shouting it at him: another insult. Then someone else shouted. "Fatherless dogs!"

And another: "Grass eaters!"

"Geldings!"

"Black sheep!"

Rusti pictured a flock of silly sheep stampeding closer, chewing as they came, and a shouty, strangled laugh burst out of him, unexpected. Then the attackers emerged out of the brightness of the sun, and he saw they were not animals of any breed, but men on horseback with swords and bows and axes.

Bandits. Not warriors. Hotheads. Don't they know about the might of Tamburlaine? Idiots. Rusti swung his sword.

Eyesight – all five senses – sharper than in all his life. Seeing everything! Faces, beaded with sweat. Smell of horse – sour breath. Scimitars. Same shape as the moon. Moon in the sky already: watching. Rusti raised his shield; heard a blade hit it: heard it with the marrow of his forearm. Something thumped his back: a limb hacked from some man's body. Not his though. *Check body. Nothing amiss – nothing missing…*

Except (he noticed) his blood had all flowed to the core of his body and his face was very cold.

Horses and ponies crowding in. Legs pinched against Arrow's ribs. Must reach open space. Two camels; riders armed with sharpened poles. Turn Arrow. Use body weight. Yah: can't catch me!

A jeering satisfaction. *Eeeeasy.*

Somewhere, a bugle. Different, louder trump close by. Elephants broken loose – milling about, encircled by the fighting. Men wrestling hand-to-hand among their legs.

Should have howdahs, and armour, and warriors up top, lobbing javelins and fire! Yowls and shrieks – war whoops and the screaming of men on the ground.

A head rolled to a halt right in his path. *No beard. Young, then.*

The skirmish was over. A few of the bandits escaped into the encroaching darkness. Most did not.

Returning to the kibitki, its poles skewed, its roof charred, Rusti was greeted by Kavita, who threw his thin arms around Rusti's neck and hugged him close. A couple of warriors riding by pointed and laughed at the sight of a slave-girl expressing her thanks for the saving of her worthless life.

Rusti, embarrassed, tried to pull free of the wiry, clinging arms, but Kavita was strong. His mouth was close to Rusti's ear and the admiration burst from him like hot steam, hissing. True, he was trembling, but not with terror. Kavita was quivering with a fierce, triumphant hysteria. His feet began to stamp, and Rusti realized he was dancing, celebrating the victory he had watched from under the folds of the fallen tent.

The inside of Kavi's head was alive with pictures. Like shadows thrown by a campfire, the pictures flared and flickered – the sweeping turn of those massed ponies, the silver forest of blades, man-and-horse made one, the colour of noise, the noise of bloodletting. All his secret thoughts had found shape. It was as if he had wished the skirmish into being. Now he saw Rusti in a new light – a hero and a warrior who could deal out death, a boy full of power, a boy as full of violence as himself.

As for Rusti, what did he remember of the skirmish? Only that head rolling into his path; the expression on its face, the look in the eyes. A young face, no older than his own. Eastern eyes, but not Mongol eyes. A foreigner – an enemy, therefore, and ripe for killing. Except that Rusti himself had such eyes.

They made the journey by elephant. Dawn was still a way off when they arrived. Kavi was a mahout once more, dress rolled up in a bundle under him and his hair wild. There might have been a joy in prancing through the moonlight, clinging to the dry wrinkles of the elephants' necks, but there was only one idea filling Rusti's head to bursting. All day he had barely spoken. All day he had thought about nothing but Zubihat. His home town.

And here it was again: a few broken walls, some neglected fields and a single tower, sticking up like an old man's last rotten tooth. Did the spirits of the Dead linger in this awful place, unable to escape their fearful fate, still reaching out imploring fingers? No wonder the locals had abandoned Zubihat. Elephants are sensitive to things invisible. Gajanan and Damini walked now as if the ground was hot, their feet hovering over stone and soil and litter, reading the story of Zubihat from the marks it had left in the earth.

"Help me," said Rusti, and Kavi gave a start. In this immense, sad silence, the smallest sound was unnerving. "Will you? *You will! You have to help me!*" demanded Rusti.

"I help."

The tower was not as tall as Rusti had expected. It was not as tall as in his dreams. Stories grow in the telling. The real thing did not touch the sky or blot out the moon. It was the work of soldiers building in a hurry, anxious to be on their way again. Besides, a great many people can be crammed into quite a small space.

In their long and brutal lives, the elephants of Delhi had been taught to do many things – to run towards men on horseback who were firing arrows, to pick their way through rubble and fire, to kneel and bellow on command. But now, their riders' commands confused them. Damini and Gajanan rested their broad foreheads against the rough brickwork of the tower, but could not understand what more was being asked of them.

Luckily, nature had planted in their great heads the instinct to uproot trees, and the instinct called to them now, as surely as if it were a voice within the tower. Both elephants leaned forwards, leaned with all their great weight, pushing – just pushing with their foreheads. There was a whispering grate of brittle pottery. The bricks had been baked in a hurry, used too new, not weathered by monsoon or sun. The mortar had been poor stuff, sloppy stuff. The builders had not been bricklayers. No architect had designed this chimney of baked mud. Now its bricks began to shift under the strain. Dust fell onto the elephants' toes, like dried blood.

With heels and sticks, Rusti and Kavi goaded them forwards again, side by side, to lean and push and strain – to barge over this unnatural, giant, lifeless tree in the dark, dark landscape. Kavi grinned at the thought of destroying something built by the Crooked One. He did not ask questions, ask, "Why?" He was simply glad. Somehow he had managed to infect Rusti with the same hatred as was raging in his own bloodstream.

A hole. A clattering tumble of bricks. The elephants snatched their delicate trunks aside and the boys covered their heads with their arms. *Bang! Bang!* Sharp corners. Rough edges. The falling bricks grazed their faces and forearms, and Kavi yelped with pain. Rusti gave a cry of both terror and triumph. The tower was breached! He felt a surge of hope, too. Maybe, if he could break down this wall, he would be able to see into the Past, glimpse the Truth, find something he had lost. There was terror, too. What would he let loose from the tower if he broke it open? Bones? Or ghosts? The walking dead? Screams or rats or a flutter of groping hands? Sweat streamed down his face, and his teeth chattered, so that Kavi asked time and again, "You want we stop?"

"Just help me, Kavi. Please. Just *help* me."

Scared to look up, in case a brick fell in his face, Rusti felt an odd compulsion, even so, to see the sky. Were those really bats? Those flickers of black? Or were they birds of ill omen? Or... The spirits of the Dead hang in the sky over the soil of their homeland: this much he knew. That meant that his mother's spirit and his father's – his *real* father's spirit – were watching him now from behind the black fleece clouds, the hangings of moonlight. What would they think of this son of theirs? A warrior in the Great Emir's army, a rider of elephants, a pretend Mongol boy masquerading as a man?

By sheer force of will, Rusti set Gajanan at the tower once more, and the elephant pressed his great forehead to the brickwork…and stove it in.

A torrent of bricks came thudding down all around, grazing Gajanan's neck and ears, sending the poor beast stumbling backwards. One brick struck Rusti in the breastbone, another the side of his head, and he fell from the elephant's shoulders onto the flat of his back. The sky above him was full of flying bricks. Gajanan's feet, stepping and overstepping him, actually tugged a lock of his hair out of his skull. The clouds milled about the ghastly moon. He could hear the sound of bricks breaking brittle bones, and feared that they were his own…

Kavi saw Rusti fetch down the tower on top of himself. He saw his friend fall, and dismounted in the blink of an eye. Stupid, reckless boy: what was he thinking of? Finding Rusti unconscious, Kavi dragged him by his feet out of the reach of falling masonry.

Now! If Rusti was dead, Kavi could go – simply ride – away from the Horde, away from Borte and captivity – away from Kavita. Good! Good, then! Let Rusti be dead!

Except that panic and grief and hope and fright kept hitting Kavi in the head like falling bricks. Why? Rusti was just a Mongol, wasn't he? Just one of the Crooked One's dogs busy eating up the world. No loss.

There again, if Kavi rode away, he would never achieve his ambition, never keep the promise he had made to himself.

Suddenly: hoof beats. Kavi felt them through the soles of his feet, long before he heard them. Horsemen! And coming his way. Mongol outriders? Or the bandits who had attacked earlier? It did not matter much either way, if they found him here, alone but for two elephants and a dead warrior.

"Rusti! Rusti, wake! Get up! Men comes!" Of course he did not want Rusti to be dead! Who else did he have in the world? Who else came to the rescue every time Death opened its jaws to eat Kavi? "Rusti up! Up!" he hissed, prodding his friend, grabbing his shirt, lifting his shoulders off the ground. Ha! Kavi could get an elephant to its feet with a word and a push, but he had no idea how to do the same with a boy! Closer and closer came the drumming hoofs.

The elephants! How could they miss seeing the elephants? Kavi ran to Gajanan and Damini and drew them coaxingly, tenderly behind the base of the tower. He had them kneel down, coiling their trunks away as if he were tucking them into bed. At night, from a distance – with luck – they might just look like an outcrop of rocks, their silhouettes broken up by fallen rubble. Then he ran back and dragged Rusti by his heels into the only hiding place he could think of – into the base of the ruined tower.

He was greeted by a smell of decay, moss and bat lime. The wall still stood to a height higher then his head, shutting out the moonlight. His groping fingers told him that the floor was piled high with smooth sticks and bricks and litter. The horsemen must be within sight of the tower by now. Kavi curled up on his knees, folding himself down till his forehead touched the ground, letting his shoulders droop.

Back in Delhi – a thousand years before (or so it seemed) – he had seen the wise men – the swamis and yogis – fold themselves away like this, to rest their souls and bodies, curled up like children in the womb. In fact Kavi could almost hear a mother's voice whispering to him now: *Lie still, child. Peace, child. All's well…*

The bandits slowed their ponies to let them breathe, and to take swigs from a pigskin flagon. They noted the tower silhouetted against the moon, and, being local men, saw that it had shrunk to a stump since the day before. Had the detested Timur-the-Lame ordered it to be pulled down? Should they take a look inside? Should they see if the stories were true? See what twelve years could do to a hundred old men, women and… They shuddered superstitiously and shared the flagon again, to get up more nerve. Then they dug their heels into their ponies' sides and trotted towards the ruin.

All of a sudden, with a soughing roar, a blue glow engulfed the broken tower. Ice-blue fire. It flared high into the sky, loosing streamers like shot silk; flapping, fluttering, luminous vapour – sapphire tongues that licked at the underside of the moon.

Superstitious dread seized the riders and spooked their ponies. The man holding the flagon dropped it, but they were far too scared to go back for it. They rode as if the ghosts of all their enemies were after them.

* * *

When Rusti came round, he found himself in a charnel house of bones. But he had dreamed it so many times before that it seemed like just another nightmare. For a long time he lay looking up at the sky, wondering how much damage the bricks had done to him. Beside him, Kavi unfolded like an exotic flower. It seemed time to tell the truth. This was no place fit for lies.

"My mother was walled up in this tower," Rusti told him. "The Chronicler told me. She pushed me out through a hole in the wall. I am a tajik like you."

A long silence greeted his confession. At last Kavi held up a long thighbone and studied it, frowning. "Your mother? She is here?"

Rusti thought about this. "No. Not now," he said. "She is *here* now." And he laid one hand over his heart.

Kavi the Mahout might have covered his own heart and thought of his own mother. Kavita said, "I am not tajik. I am slave."

Outside, their elephant Gajanan pulled herself to her feet and, in brushing against the tower, dislodged another shower of bricks.

"Why did you drag me in here?" said Rusti, both arms shielding his head. "Safer outside."

So Kavi told him about the riders, and about the need to hide. And Rusti said that Kavi was not slave at all, but a friend – a good friend. The best.

Once – a thousand years before – Kavi the Mahout might have smiled and pressed his palms together and bowed his thanks. "Kavita the Slave" only threw aside the thighbone, sniffed his fingers and pulled a face. He looked round at the dreadful remains, and mentally added another crime to Tamburlaine's account. "I help you," he said. "Now you help me."

"Help you?" said Rusti. "Help you escape, you mean?"

Kavita shook his head, long hair spilling round his face, wild as madness. "No. No. Help kill Crooked Pig. Soon. One day. We kill him. Yes?"

One week later, the white tent of the Royal Chronicler was pitched once more among the others in the Royal Enclosure. Rusti was sent for once again, to play chess. And yet, when he arrived, there was no sign of the chessboard.

"I have been absent," said Shidurghu. "My duties took me another way."

"I know," said Rusti, feeling clever. "You had to act as the Emir's interpreter. Because you come from these parts, don't you?"

The Chronicler's face twisted into a knot of surprise or irritation. "No! Who says so? Not at all. It is a lie. I know the language, but I know many languages! The Mighty Lord of the Fortunate Conjunction requires it!"

Rusti pulled his lips between his teeth and bit down hard, vowing not to open his mouth ever again and risk saying the wrong thing. He dared not even leave, despite the terrible silence cramming the tent, the old man still seemed on the verge of speaking. Sure enough:

"I must chronicle all that happened while I was gone. Perhaps you can help me. Did anything happen of which I should make note?"

"Me?" Rusti's face burned. Why would the old man ask him…unless he knew… Unless he suspected. Unless he could read minds.

"You saw the tower? At Zubihat?"

Rusti's mouth turned dry in the instant. He licked his lips and nodded, but seeing that the old man's eyelids were closed, had to force himself to do more than nod. "I saw," he said.

"Are they not magnificent, the works of the Great Emir? Has he not left his mark on the world of men?"

Rusti swallowed. He had no idea what he was supposed to say. He thought it might choke him to agree. So he just repeated: "I saw." When Shidurghu showed no sign of opening his eyes or of continuing the conversation, Rusti backed towards the door. His hand was on the tent flap when the old man mumbled something:

"They say that at night blue flames rise from its summit. High into the sky. Heatless blue flames. Is this true?"

"Not any more." It fell out of Rusti's mouth, unstoppable as an egg from a duck.

The old man's pale eyes snapped open. They bored into Rusti, prising more words out of him like it or not.

"It fell down. The tower. A bit. Well, quite a lot. Fell down."

"Truly?" Shidurghu could not disguise his astonishment.

"Lightning I expect!" lied Rusti, on the spur of the moment. "Or maybe a stampede ran into it! Buffalo. Or deer. Or camels! You could write that down in your History."

Shidurghu closed his eyes again and released Rusti from their alarming gaze. Awkwardly the boy backed out – remembering not to turn his back! – keeping his eye fixed on the unpredictable writer-down of History.

So he saw the old man whisper, in words intended for no one else to hear: *"The wonder of elephants!"* as a single tear crept down the papery, yellow cheek.

They planned all kinds of ways to murder the Emir. That is to say, Kavita planned and Rusti pointed out why the plans would not work. Kavita thought of pits with sharpened spikes in the bottom.

"A bodyguard always rides in front of him," said Rusti.

Kavita thought of poison.

"He has a food taster," said Rusti.

Kavita thought of setting the royal kibitki alight.

"His hounds would bark when you got close," said Rusti. "Or his leopard would eat you."

"So I sit on him with elephants!"

And Rusti laughed, because there is something comical about the idea of an elephant sitting down on a king.

Chapter Eleven

Samarqand

The Horde pitched camp on the Rose-mine Plain, outside the walls of Samarqand – a velvety expanse of vivid green grass crossed by two roads as straight as the flight of arrows. Along these roads came messengers, at a gallop, carrying dispatches for the Emir, delivering his letters and summonses. In Samarqand, his fortune-tellers would read Tamburlaine's horoscope and advise him how to become still more powerful in the coming year. His wives would show him the latest children born to him. His spies would report on rebellions or quarrels, plots or corruption in the four corners of the world.

With every passing hour, hundreds more kibitkis went up as the Horde reached its capital city –

thousands of molehills sprouting on the smoothest of lawns. There was an air of excitement, delight, celebration. The Horde had survived another campaign (those who were not dead). They had arrived home much richer (except for those who had lost everything). They had distinguished themselves as heroes (those who had not been maimed for thieving or beheaded for cowardice). They had been at war and bought themselves some peace. Now they were home for a rest.

They would not stay long, of course: nothing would induce them to settle down. They would not grow soft, like the tradesmen and slaves and craftsmen who lived here all year round. But they had been on the rout, and they deserved a little comfort. Now was the time to turn loot into hard cash and put it to good use, feasting.

Borte dismantled her chain mail of spoons and sconces, bits, stirrups, whistles and inkwells, daggers, sheaths, gauntlets and spearheads and belt buckles. She was in a hurry to get her plunder to the market before neighbours could fetch down the value with their own hoard of looted trinkets. She raged with grief at finding she had lost the golden bracelet, prize of her collection, and a wedding gift from Cokas.

"We'll sell that pony of yours, too," she said, polishing a copper beaker she had pillaged from Delhi.

"Arrow?" Did she mean Rusti to go on foot in future? She had already sold Rusti's old pony to a neighbour whose horse had dropped dead on the trail.

"What d'you need horseflesh like that for? You can buy some cheap nag and use what's left for supplies. How else do you mean to pay? In Delhi you got nothing worth having, did you? Well, did you?" She paused for breath before throwing one last jibe at her tajik husband. "At least we shall finally see the back of those vile elephants!"

"My elephants?" The thought had never occurred to Rusti.

"*Your* elephants?" spat Borte contemptuously. "Is that what they are? Have you told the Grand Emir? Go on, then! Drive them to market and sell them. *Your* elephants, indeed! Be sure and hold out for a good price, won't you? *Your* elephants. Huh!"

Rusti, who tried never to meet his wife's eye, looked across at her now – at the sneer on her sour, shrewish face – and thought, *If the royal elephants stay in Samarqand, I'll stay too.* An absurd thought, of course, but he could not imagine passing the creatures over into the care of anyone else.

Borte was right. The Emir's zoo was here, his collection of exotic beasts, his curiosities. Rusti had only ever been an escort, delivering the Emir's captives into the charge of the royal zookeepers. On the trail, elephants were a nuisance. They served no purpose. Camels can pull carts. Horses carry a man into battle. Greyhounds and leopards can be used for hunting. But elephants? The generals did not want them for weapons. The quartermasters said they ate too much. They were good for nothing but the Royal Zoo, or maybe one of the Emir's circuses.

Rusti got to his feet, angry and miserable. Borte demanded to know where he was going.

"To see the elephants. They'll need cleaning up – getting ready. Come, Kavita. You can help me."

"Oh no you don't," Borte told him, grabbing their slave by the wrist and dragging him over the threshold. Outside she took hold of a hank of hair and manhandled Kavita towards the ponies. "I need her to carry my saleables."

Rusti took hold of Kavita's other wrist. "And I need her to help deliver the elephants," he retaliated.

For a moment, he thought Borte would make it a tug of war and that Kavi would have his arms pulled out of their sockets. But his wife's desire to be rid of the elephants must have outweighed her need for someone to bully. Borte let go, spat on the ground and said, "Maybe we can trade *her* for a girl that doesn't stink of elephants."

Rusti really did need Kavi's help with the elephants: he could never have steered them through the busy city streets single-handedly. He still did not know how he was going to part with them. Borte knew that. So she rode alongside them all the way to the zoo. There was no chance for the friends to talk, no chance for Rusti to apologize for parting the little mahout from his giant friends. The elephants were Kavi's last link with Delhi. In parting with Gaurang and Mahamati, Phoolenda, Gajanan and Mumu, he would have to stop being Kavi the Mahout and become Kavita ever more. Rusti would just have to be a better friend to Kavita, once the elephants were gone.

The Emir's zoo was a sordid patch of ground amid the other splendours of the city. A smell of rotting meat and blood hung in the air. The bones of carcasses fed to the meat-eaters lay everywhere, like the relics of a massacre. The elephants baulked at the smell, the melancholy, the fear, the noise, the sickness in the air. Their trunks coiled in revulsion. Their ears lay close against their heads. Rusti did his best for them. He repeated over and over again the quantity of hay his beasts would need, the amount of water, and gave instructions on how to tend their hides. But the zookeepers were not listening. They simply gaped and marvelled, and all they took in was the bigness of elephants. "No, no! Not meat-eaters!" wailed Rusti distractedly: "HAY!" Meanwhile, Borte looked on with disgust, and complained that time was wasting: she had valuable loot to sell.

As for Kavi, he watched with dull, blank eyes. He did not, like Rusti, wipe away shaming tears with the heel of one hand. He did not say "goodbye", as Rusti did, to each animal in turn. "Goodbye Phoolenda. Goodbye Alpa. Goodbye Mumu—" The sadness of the moment hardly touched home at all, because there was a hate inside Kavita's head larger than all these elephants put together.

Worn down by Borte's nagging, they left the zoo and headed for the markets. The streets of Samarqand were crammed with foreigners, tradesmen and Tamburlaine's Horde. The home comers had been celebrating ever since reaching the Rose-mine Plain, and were mostly drunken, reeling, loud and loutish. Bodies collided. Tables were rummaged and knocked askew. But the tradesmen went on smiling, hands clasped over their stomachs, nodding a welcome, mouthing a blessing, commending their wonderful arrays of fruit, shoes, perfume, sweets and silk scarves.

The merchants who had come to *buy*, on the other hand, shook their heads and ran sad eyes over the loot laid in front of them. They pushed out their lips, wrinkled their noses and sucked their teeth.

"So many of these."

"Such poor stuff."

"No demand."

"Not worth a chicken feather."

They bought, but they paid next to nothing.

"Do you know the trouble I will have selling this?"

"Two stirrups yes, but one?"

Borte raged and cursed and threatened the merchants, but they had heard it all before – the stories of daring and hardship. For an hour, she refused to sell any of her loot at such low prices, barging Kavita onwards ahead of her, a hand on the slave's neck. Burdened down with the heavy basket of loot, Kavita staggered and stumbled. On and on the three of them went, from table to table, through the paved squares, the crowded parks, into the slave market where an auctioneer was selling a different kind of loot: the girls and women enslaved at Delhi.

A hapless peasant was selling flowers out of the panniers on his balding donkey. "A present for your lovely wife!" he called out to Rusti. "No thorns, guaranteed! A rose for your sweetheart! One also for your mother there!"

Borte might not have noticed the insult at all if Rusti had not laughed. He should never have laughed, but the *completeness* of the mistake was too much for him: a boy mistaken for his wife, his wife mistaken for his mother. The joke fizzed down his nose like sherbet, and he gave a great shouty laugh. Borte grabbed the rose out of the vendor's hand – and promptly impaled herself on the thorns guaranteed not to be there. Then even Kavita the Silent, Kavita the Sad showed his teeth in a helpless, sniggering grin.

Borte punched the donkey. The donkey set off to run. The rose seller went after it, calling on his ancestors to snap the poles of Borte's kibitki and let it fall on her and all her relations. The two boys laughed even more, hysterical in the stifling heat. They pushed each other, told each other to stop, but the laughter just kept coming. Borte, hot and frustrated, had bruised one hand on the donkey and scratched the other on the rose. So she did not lash out with her fists. She did not scream at Rusti that he was a tajik and a fool. She simply looked around for a way to wipe the smiles off their faces. What she would give to be rid of that thin, black-eyed, jet-haired slave-girl Rusti took such a delight in!

So she gave the corner of Kavita's shawl into the grasp of the auctioneer. "Sell this one," she said.

"Half to you, half to me," said the slave merchant, but Borte no longer cared about getting a good deal. She just yearned to do something spiteful.

"NO!" said Rusti.

"She's a strong worker. Strong like a man," Borte told the auctioneer; she was the one wearing the grin now.

The market square was rainbow-hued with Delhi's womenfolk, their wailing and sobbing buried dune-deep now under months of misery on the trail. They were so far sunk into despair that they seemed barely curious about what new unhappiness lay in store for them. Only those with sisters or mothers still alive clung to them for fear they would be parted for ever.

"I forbid it," said Rusti. "I need her for the..."

Borte's grin widened. "Elephants? But the elephants are gone, aren't they?"

Prospective buyers were poking and prodding the

slaves on sale, staring into their mouths to judge their ages. "Do you not *want* help with your work, woman?" Rusti demanded, but his voice came out whining and peevish.

"With the profit from your horse, I can buy better," said Borte. "A big Syrian boy for me. A big, handsome, Syrian boy."

"I am not selling Arrow!"

"Why? What do *you* want with a good horse, *tajik*? Sell the one you stole, and buy some nag instead. A slave for me and a nag for you."

The auctioneer broke off from shouting his wares, amused by the squabble. Then he gave a tug on Kavita's shawl and toppled him in among the other slaves.

"Not for sale!" shouted Rusti, but the man shrugged, suggesting he could not hear for all the noise. "If he tries to sell her, I will buy her back!" Rusti told his wife, but she only snorted with contempt.

"Listen to your mother, boy. Mothers know best," advised the auctioneer, and Borte abruptly stopped laughing.

Kavi, who lived every day on a knife-edge of fear, felt the knife cut deep. A new owner would soon find out his secret. Would-be buyers were crowding round, groping and squeezing the goods on sale, like cooks buying peaches or plums. A woman pinched his biceps. Would it be here, then? Was today the day that had been hurtling towards him all along? The day when he would be found out? Was this where he would meet his end, trodden underfoot like a rotten orange, in a foreign marketplace?

The slave merchant completed a sale – three girls bought by a skinner to scrape animal pelts and dye leather. The other girls, like bright fish in a pool, moved sharply away, trying to reach the rear of the shoal, stay out of sight, avoid the eyes of customers. And suddenly the skinner had hold of Kavi by the hair. "I'll take this one too," he said.

"Not for sale!" shouted Rusti, and the crowd laughed, thinking they understood: a favourite slave-girl: a jealous wife. The skinner ran his hands over Kavita's back to judge whether the slave-girl had been well fed.

"What are you bidding?" the auctioneer wanted to know.

"Not for sale!" repeated Rusti, and his wife kicked him.

"Ten," said the skinner.

"Twenty," said a butcher in the crowd, thinking how he would put the girl to work on the offal first and let her work her way up to jointing and filleting.

"I was given her by the Gungal Emir!" Rusti protested, knowing no one was listening. All these girls had been gifts from Tamburlaine to his men, hadn't they?

"Twenty-five," said the skinner, but his eyes trailed towards a more shapely girl. He would not go higher than twenty-five.

"Thirty!" bawled the butcher.

"I hate you, Borte," said Rusti. "He was my friend."

"He? Who?" said Borte, bewildered but unmoved.

"Sixty!" The bid came from the back of the crowd, and everyone turned round with a babble of astonishment, to see who was squandering such wealth on a scrawny, shapeless slave-girl. There sat a man astride a white saddlecloth, his helmet and horse's bridle trimmed with ermine: a sure sign of rank. His heels nudged his horse forwards, and the crowd parted respectfully to let him through.

Kavi's hands clenched into fists, then opened limply again. Was it Fate, this armoured figure moving towards him with a bagful of coins? Kavi raised one arm, and the rider lifted him onto the horse. The bag of money passed to the auctioneer.

Borte gave a crow of pleasure at this unexpected

luck. Casting not one glance at Kavita (with whom she had shared a tent for a year) she began quarrelling with the auctioneer about his cut of the money. Only out of the corner of her eye did she see her husband take off and run.

Rusti ran after the man on the horse, dodging round people, jumping over small children and dogs, straining to keep the white-brimmed helmet in sight. The crowds gave way to the horse, but not to Rusti. He had to run the entire length of the camel market, the lane of potteries, the Park of Good Fortune, the Palace of the Queens, and his lungs were empty of air before he drew level, outside the paper factory. "Please! Please wait! Mistake!" he panted, taking hold of a stirrup and the boot within it.

Both rider and Kavi looked down at him, their faces impassive, watching him struggle to catch his breath.

"...pay more!" he gasped. "...buy back. Seventy. Eighty! Horse! Got a horse! Worth plenty!"

A fly settled on the horseman's cheek. He waved away the fly, or possibly the boy holding his boot. "I was sent," he said, as if words were too costly to lavish on the likes of Rusti. "I follow orders. I buy."

"Who? Who sent you? I'll ask him!"

The horseman seemed too bored to do more than smirk. Life had taught him only to oblige those above him in rank.

"He buys for me," said a voice, and all three looked up. At an upper window of the paper factory stood Shidurghu, the Royal Chronicler, his arms filled with sheaves of paper. "You, girl. Come up here. Carry these for me."

Wordless, Kavi slid from the horse and climbed the stairs to take the old man's purchase from him. On the staircase Kavita looked like someone swimming upwards from the seabed.

In front of a stranger, Rusti could not object. And he could hardly offer Shidurghu his own pony, in payment. The old man flicked a coin – its shine spun out of the shadows and landed at Rusti's feet. What, did he think Rusti was: a beggar?

"She was not for sale," said Rusti, leaving the coin on the ground.

"Read it," said Shidurghu in his high, querulous voice.

Rusti looked down at the coin lying in the dirt. He knew the meaning of the three circles stamped into the metal: they were the fortunate conjunction of planets that had marked Tamburlaine's birth. There were words, too, on the coin. But what were words to the likes of Rusti?

Shidurghu and his new slave turned away indoors, and passed into the dark.

Chapter Twelve

Circus

A circus. The prospect raised everyone's spirits, though few would be invited. A niece of the Gungal Emir was to be married, and marriages need celebrating. What better than to float apples in the water fountains, loose songbirds from rooftop wicker cages, hang up flags in the streets? And put on a circus!

A circus calls for animals – not just acrobats and clowns and daredevil riders but animals, both real and pretend. The Royal Zoo was thrown into panic and confusion. For whatever way the zookeepers turned, they fell over elephants. No cage was big enough to hold them. They had been penned into a paddock but within the hour they had "leaned" the fences flat. These saggy, raddled giants from Delhi were perpetually thirsty, so that they roamed about supping water from any trough, anywhere. Perpetually hungry, they walked out of the barren compounds in search of food, pulling up the delicate little trees and shrubs in the royal parks, plucking the apples out of the fountains and dislodging the flags with their tusks. Unscrubbed and unoiled, they had begun to pick up parasites from the other beasts in the zoo and, scratching themselves against its pillars, brought down the portico of a government building.

The zookeepers tried hobbling the elephants, chaining big chocks of wood round their ankles. All but the smallest, the calf, only dragged the chocks away with them, smashing a whole row of terracotta urns standing outside the potteries, before returning in a mob to the zoo.

What was needed was an expert handler. What was needed was the boy who had delivered the Emir's elephants to the zoo! But how to find him? Impossible! He had disappeared into the teeming chaos of the Rose-mine and its six thousand kibitkis, and they did not even know his name.

Luckily, another boy turned up.

It was as if he had fallen out of the sky in answer

to the zookeepers' prayers. A dark-skinned, doe-eyed Indian boy was spotted one day standing in among the elephants, rubbing balm into the chain burns on their monstrous ankles. And when the zookeepers discovered that he could make the elephants obey him, they were overjoyed. The boy had been sent (he said) by the Emir himself, to prepare the animals for the wedding circus. Who were they to argue?

Many animals appeared in the circuses of Samarqand: cheetahs and monkeys, lions and horses, bears and camels. Not all of them were the real thing. Elaborate costumes stitched from split-skin and dyed to outlandish colours were brought out of storage and softened with vegetable oil and by beating. On the day before the royal wedding, the tiring tent, where the costumes were stored, looked like the scene of some dreadful atrocity. The limp and sorry bodies of animals were apparently being beaten mercilessly with flails. But as fur flew, the hide softened. Meanwhile, acrobats and clowns limbered up and practised their dances, complaining of the heat. Next day they would wriggle into their animal suits and cavort about for the entertainment of the royal guests.

The twin brothers, who wore the orange camel suit, were quarrelling about who would be the front and who the back half. They had been quarrelling for years. Their mother, who stitched them into the suit before each performance, blamed the bad-tempered nature of camels: said anger had rubbed off on them from the camel hide. (They were certainly both fond of spitting.)

Rusti passed them on his way into the city to visit the elephants. He did not pay much attention. An elephant, once it has arrived, occupies a very great space in a boy's life, and the disappearance of Tamburlaine's elephants from Rusti's life had left him as hollow as one of those empty carnival suits swinging in the sunshine. Kavi, too, had left an emptiness.

The sight of the elephants instantly lifted his spirits. The anxious, rheumy-eyed beasts he had last seen milling unhappily about, frightened and bewildered, were transformed. They had been washed and oiled, then painted with swirling patterns of indigo paint. From the tips of their indigo trunks to their absurdly stringy tails, wound in gold cord, they were magnificent, exotic, monumental. They filled Rusti with awe, as gods might if they arrived unexpectedly one day at your door.

And best of all, there was Kavi! Not Kavita, no, but Kavi! He was pushing handfuls of shrivelled apples into the mouth of Gaurang and Alpa, Mahamati, Gajanan and the rest. His hands and forehead were also stained blue with indigo.

"Kavi! *Kavi!*" called Rusti and, in his heart, he thanked the old Chronicler over and over. Now the elephants would be tended properly. Now Kavi would be freed of his disguise. "Kavi! Over here!" Rusti had wanted the job himself. But now at least he could come here and help, and all would be well between old friends. "Kavi!"

But Kavi did not come. It was Mumu who recognized Rusti's voice and came running over, reading his face, leaving blue kisses on his cheeks with the tip of her scarred trunk. The calf followed her, out of curiosity; the calf's mother was close behind. Then Kavi was obliged to come to the edge of the field and to hoick them away with his mahout's stick.

"Go away, Rusti," he said in an undertone. "Alone I do."

Panic nudged Rusti in the chest: "Does the History Man know you are here? Did you run away?"

"No. He know. All is good. Go now."

But Rusti did not go, of course. He explained his

new plans: how he had decided not to go back on the trail. He was going to stay in Samarqand. Let Borte go. Let the others go. He would stay and help Kavi tend the elephants.

"No. I am good. Not need you. Alone I do."

"What about the promise? You made me promise to help you..."

"I need you not. Go away."

And something collapsed inside Rusti, like a mud brick tower, and he felt robbed and cheated and miserable. It was good, wasn't it, that Kavi no longer wanted to murder Tamburlaine? That was sensible. Why then did Rusti feel so unwanted, so unnecessary? Because Kavi had taken from him all the things that made him special: his elephants, his place in the white kibitki, and his role as Tamburlaine's elephant boy. "Why are they blue?" he asked flatly, trying not to resent Kavi. "Are they going to the wedding circus?"

At last the little mahout beamed. "Oh yes!" And a flash of light went through his eyes as bright as summer lightning. For some reason, Rusti was very, very scared by that lightning flash.

* * *

The Royal Chronicler had a home in the city – beside the library that housed the journals of Nasir al-Din Tusi, Zafar-nama of Sharaf al-Din Yazdi and all the other great writers-down of History. The guards did not want to let him in, but Rusti told them he had come to play chess. He had to know if Kavi had been truly freed from slavery. If his friend had simply run away, there would be a death sentence on his head, men searching the city for him to burn him alive as an example to other would-be runaways.

"I have no taste for games today, boy," said Shidurghu when Rusti entered. The old man's hands moved in a flutter over his desk, as if the boy's arrival had alarmed him.

"I have to talk to you, sir," Rusti insisted. "About that slave, Kavi."

Shidurghu waved a hand. "All is well. He has my permission."

"But—"

"A man should do what he does best. My slave – my ex-slave, I should say – has a skill with elephants. In Samarqand live many races. In a city a foreigner may fade into obscurity, lose himself. Look at me, for example..." He picked up a coin from the desk and turned it over and over between finger and thumb.

"So he didn't run away? He's allowed? You did set him free? "

"Free. What is that? The Mongol Empire is, you might say, a large net full of fish. The fish may swim to and fro. They may fool themselves that they are at liberty. But ultimately their fate is sealed. Things other than chains bind us, lad. Duty. Oaths. Gratitude." The coin clicked down on the desk and Shidurghu invited Rusti to pick it up. Rusti stepped backwards. Again the coin: its three lucky planets, its three words. Kavita had cost sixty. Why was Rusti worth only one? It would appear that the Chronicler had finished with him. He had served some purpose without knowing it, then been dismissed like a beggar, with the offer of one coin. How dare Shidurghu stir up all those feelings with his story of towers and babies and golden bracelets, and then take Kavi instead!

"Do you wish to go to the wedding circus?" said Shidurghu unexpectedly. The offer must have surprised even him, for he seemed about to take it back. Then he thumped the desk with a clenched fist and said, "Yes! You should. You should see!" And rose stiffly and walked over to an ottoman chest and took out a wedding shawl. As he laid the band of brilliant embroidered silk around Rusti's shoulders, his long pale trembling hands seemed loath to let go of the cloth. Then he enclosed Rusti's head, just for an instant, in a grip of steel, before pushing him bodily out of the door.

As soon as Borte saw the wedding shawl, she tugged it from round his neck. *Maybe she means to sell that too,* thought Rusti.

"This is mine. What will you wear?" she said, admiring her reflection in a polished metal pot.

The prospect was certainly thrilling: a place at the ringside, along with the officers and ministers and chroniclers and chamberlains and wives and bodyguards of the Grand Emir, Lord of the Fortunate Conjunction. Rusti would see the bride and groom – the clowns and acrobats – dancers and daredevils! His elephants, too. But Rusti was still shaking from his encounter with the Chronicler, still struggling to make sense of the coin, the shawl, the push.

Borte combed the dry skin out of her eyebrows, oiled her hair and bound a silk scarf so tightly over her nose that the veins stood out around her eyes. A small nose might be the mark of beauty in a woman, thought Rusti, but a purple pulse throbbing in her forehead probably wasn't.

"I am going alone," he told her, but she ignored him as completely as she ignored the flies sipping the oil off her hair.

In the event, the scene was so chaotic that, seeing Rusti's wife cleaved to his side and wearing the marriage-guest gift, no one challenged his own right to be there: the one shawl allowed in two guests. On their way in, they passed the tiring tent and caught a glimpse of dancing boys climbing naked into their animal – and bird – suits. They had left it to the last moment to put on the sweltering costumes. Puzzled by one ugly brown costume with large flapping ears, Rusti realized that it was someone's idea of an elephant.

Their fellow guests smelled of koumis and sweat and rotten meat. The circus smelled of tarry torch smoke, horses and attar of roses. Banners hung limp, firecrackers dangled.

Borte sat herself down on a bench right at the front, and Rusti sat down too, trying to look as if it had been his idea from the start. They were soon sandwiched between a magistrate and an ambassador from Georgia. For an hour nothing happened, and the audience snacked on rumour: the Emir was ill! The bride had quarrelled with the groom! A meteor storm had been seen in the sky, presaging bad luck! But there was no truth in any of it. The wedding party arrived amid wild cheering and quacking music, the Emir looking as tiny and crooked as ever, but beaming with delight, holding hands with the lovely Cholpan-Mulk-agha, his favourite wife.

And there, lacking a wedding shawl, of course, but close to the high, red seat of Tamburlaine, Shidurghu the Chronicler sat, to witness yet another memorable day and to record it for future generations. His face was as pale as parchment paper, and Rusti could not read it. The bride was presented with a gift of white birds in a box, which she meekly released – so meekly in fact that the doves stayed inside the box and had to be poked into flight with a stick.

The pretend animals cavorted about on stilts, pushing their heads into baskets, knocking off hats, frightening small children. A "panther" stalked something with long soft ears and killed it in a kind of tragic ballet. The real animals flinched and shied away from the noise, the fires, the seething press of people. Led in on chains, they hung back fearfully, showing the whites of their eyes.

A clown cracked a whip playfully around the ears of the pretend animals. He caught an "elephant" a nasty flick on the ear and the elephant (who had been drinking since morning) came after him – launched a punch and missed (hampered by being up on stilts), then lost his balance and fell over. The clown knocked him unconscious with the butt of his whip. Those who saw it roared with joy. Tamburlaine himself gripped the arms of his chair and bared a jumble of brown teeth, and his shoulders jerked with mirth.

Was this the man whose praise had meant so much to Rusti? This man who built towers? If Shidurghu was truly a man of Zubihat, how could he bear to sit meekly by, scribing words in praise of this man? He ought to hate Tamburlaine just as much as Kavi did.

Another clown tied a string of firecrackers to the tail of a pretend donkey and lit them. The donkey brayed and bucked and kicked up his hind legs. Easy to forget there were people inside. Clever. Funny (though the sudden flash and banging had scared Rusti).

Too much like lightning.

The daylight gradually choked on the black smoke from the thousand torches. The sky blackened into evening. The moon grew silver enough to sell in a Samarqand market. The crack cavalrymen brought their tricks to a close and an evening breeze blew in a strange smell, and a cacophony of animal noises. The

Emir's only remaining rhinoceros got away from its keepers and trotted through the crowd scattering wedding guests.

Tamburlaine chortled with glee. Rusti wished the rhinoceros would turn its single horn on the Gungal Emir and toss him over the moon. But of course the monster came to a halt, dazzled and confused in the empty arena. Its keepers fell on the eight chains trailing from its tusk and feet and throat and, after a moment or two, dragged it away.

Now the elephants were coming! Rusti could glimpse them emerging from the darkness, the crowds parting to give them passage. They set their feet down so gently that they made no sound, only welled into view, like sea breakers. In their indigo splendour they looked utterly magnificent. There was something about all those inky loops and coils that put Rusti in mind of Shidurghu's writing, his secret code. What would Rusti have written if he had properly mastered reading and writing? What would he have written on the huge vellum of an elephant? Anything! Since the Great Emir could not read. Anything at all! Inside his head, Rusti began to compose the poem he would paint on an elephant if he were still to own one…

The Gungal Emir Tamburlaine,
Bringer of sorrow, bringer of pain,
Cruel and ugly and stupid and vain,
Let him be drowned in a puddle of rain!

"Her!" Borte's shove pushed Rusti off his bench. "There! Look! See? Her!"

And there was Kavi, perched up on the neck of Gaurang, in a turban of indigo silk. "Look, you turnip! Are you blind? It's your…your… It's our… It's *Kavita*!"

For a whole year Borte had shared a kibitki with Kavita without ever looking carefully enough to see through the disguise. Now, by moonlight, on a smoke-filled evening and at a great distance, seeing him bare-chested and sitting astride an elephant, she recognized the features of her husband's slave.

"Yes," said Rusti, because he was busy thinking there ought to be *two* elephant boys riding into the light: Rusti and Kavi.

Baffled at first, astounded by the deception that had been practised on her, Borte could only cluck and fret like a chicken. What did it mean? Someone had cheated: it followed that she had lost out somehow, missed a trick, been deprived of some opportunity. "It's her! She's a *boy*!" was all she could find to say.

Rusti fixed his eyes on Kavi and willed him to look round. But it was too far and, besides, Kavi's eyes were fastened on the royal dais, on the royal chair.

And suddenly – like a bolt of lightning, it struck Rusti. He knew that he was looking not at Kavi the Mahout, but at Kavita with her soul of steel.

And he knew what she was planning.

What to do? What to do? Rusti sat wedged between his wife – "It's her! It's a boy!" – and the diplomat from Georgia, sweating prodigiously in a quilted coat. They were almost directly opposite the royal dais, separated from it by a wilderness of monkeys.

A dancing girl waving a ribbon on a stick had attracted the attentions of a monkey. It had grabbed the ribbon and was sitting with the end clamped between its teeth. The girl tugged. The monkey pulled back.

Rusti drew out his picture – the one he carried inside his clothes: the Chronicler's sketch of the tower at Zubihat. Rolled inside it was the pen Shidurghu had broken and let fall to the floor of his tent. Its sharpened point was clogged with dried ink. *No ink. No ink to draw with!* But by filling his mouth with spit and dipping the quill tip into his own saliva Rusti brought the dried ink back to life. It trickled down his chin. It dyed his lips purple. The taste was purple, too, with minerals and herbs and crushed beetles. But Rusti did not draw beetles.

He drew a red chair – a blobby head, a scratchy crown. He drew an elephant – trunk, legs, ears and mahout. If he had just learned to write, he could have written – *"assassin!"*

Or *"beware!"*

Or *"elephant!"*

Or *"trample!"*

Instead, he had to draw a picture of his own. He drew the red chair toppled, the Lord of the Fortunate Conjunction lying helpless on his back, Gaurang's stumpy feet poised over the Gungal Emir ready to crush the life out of him.

A tug of war was still going on between the monkey and the girl with the ribbon stick.

"Girl! Hey, girl!" called Rusti, and the girl came instantly, bowing to him. (Astonishing. Rubbing shoulders with diplomats and noblemen had turned him into a man of rank.)

"What are you doing?" Borte jabbed him in the side. Was her fool of a husband about to disgrace her again?

"Take this to the Royal Chronicler – there. Yonder! The man with…" Over and over again, he explained to the girl, so that there could be no mistake. If the note fell into the wrong hands, death and disaster would follow. The girl pranced off, carrying the parchment that might prevent a nightmare. Bombarded by monkeys, dodging the fallen torch-stands, smiling a broad, bright smile that never wavered, the dancing girl approached the benches where the Emir's closest, most trusted, most important guests sat. She wasted no time, because out of the corner of her eye, she could see the elephants starting forward into the ring, and they terrified her.

Rusti held his breath.

Shidurghu took the creased and battered scroll from the girl's upstretched hands, unrolled it, examined his fingertips as the ink stained them. His face was so pale. Looking at the scrawl, the old man turned the paper round, turned his head to one side. Then he looked directly over at Rusti – no searching the crowd: he knew just where to look. Eyes pale as snow; face pale as death.

And he smiled and nodded and crumpled the paper between both hands, and gave the girl a coin, a single coin, for her pains.

Yes, said the nod. *You are right. You have guessed rightly.*

And like a bolt of lightning it struck Rusti: his picture had told Shidurghu nothing the old man did not already know. Shidurghu had not innocently opened his doors to a little assassin. He had deliberately recruited Kavi. They were accomplices. They were twin assassins united by a single cause: to trample Emir Tamburlaine under the feet of his own elephants.

Chapter Thirteen

Little Elephant

Somehow, Rusti wriggled out from between wife and Georgian. Borte grabbed pieces of him – his hair, his sleeve, his ankle – "Where do you think you are going, you oaf?" – but he prised himself free, stepping along the back of the bench, stepping on ambassadors and the gentry of Samarqand.

He willed the elephants not to enter the ring, but even as he reached the end of the bench, their great shadows flickered past the circling torches. Gaurang entered the light, leading a cavalcade of elephants embellished in purple and gold. The wedding crowd drew in a single breath.

Another elephant – a puny, cloth elephant – lay on the ground: Rusti almost fell over it. It was the stilt-walker, knocked unconscious by the clown. The stilt-walker was still dead to the world. It is hard to wrestle an unconscious man out of an elephant costume. But Rusti managed it. He had no idea how to balance on stilts – his would be a very *short* elephant – but he managed somehow to wriggle into the sweaty, tatty, itchy costume and clutch it close around him. His rear end dragged in the dirt. It could not be helped.

Already Kavi was steering his elephants into position, circling the open space in front of the red dais. All evening the crowd, straining for a better view, had been creeping forward so that the circus ring grew smaller and smaller. Now they recoiled in superstitious dread: the circus ring widened like a startled eye.

Faster now the elephants circled, trunk-holding-tail, heel-toe, heel-toe. The little mahout astride the largest gave no visible signals, but the beasts obeyed like well-drilled soldiers, their walk breaking into a run. On the red dais, Shidurghu got up and moved closer to the Emir. The Royal Bodyguards eyed him warily, but not so warily as they eyed the elephants, who were running now, faster, all the time faster. Think what might happen if the elephant rider were to lose control…!

Suddenly another elephant entered the ring – a puny, cloth elephant, all head and no body. It was not even up on stilts, so that its cloth rump dragged along the ground. It hesitated for a moment – had to jump aside as the elephants hurtled round the ring. The crowds hardly noticed, mesmerized by the swirl of purple patterning and the trembling of the ground under their seats. The Lord of the Fortunate Conjunction leaned forward in his throne, teeth bared in rapt fascination.

Then the little cloth elephant was dancing and capering clumsily across the ring towards the dais, shouting and jeering:

"Hee hee hee, can't catch me!

I'm the King of the Elephants, see!"

Someone in the crowd laughed.

Inside the elephant head it was hot – hot as terror – and very difficult to see.

Inside the elephant-*rider*'s head it was hot – hot as madness and hatred and terror, all three. Kavi dug his hooked stick into the softness of Gaurang's neck and turned her towards the red dais. Now! Now, he was a warrior! Once – a long age before – he had ridden

Mumu into battle – his first battle – and proved nothing but a feeble failure of a boy. But now he was a warrior – a killer. Hadn't these Mongol jackals taught him that Life is War? That fighting and killing are all that matters? Are what turn a boy into a man? Well, now he had learned his lesson! Now he would trample the Crooked Pig Emir and all his ministers! Flatten them like a grove of bamboo! Crush them like eggs under a hammer! Grind their bones into the Rose-mine! Tamburlaine only *thought* he had conquered the City of Gems. Now he would find victory turning to bitterest defeat, because, in his vanity, he had taken captive Delhi's elephants. Now they would cut *him* down for it, Kavi and his elephants. A red heat-haze of horror and hate and fear blinded Kavi to everything except the scarlet chair and the demon who sat smugly smiling there. Through it all, though, he became faintly aware of a voice:

"Hee hee hee, can't catch me!

I'm the King of the Elephants, see!"

Some of the crowd were laughing. Let them! In a moment laughter would turn to broken glass in their throats! But what was that shape standing directly in front of the red dais, jigging from foot to foot like a fool? What was it supposed to be? A trunk, two ears and a body like an empty sock. Kavi could make nothing of it – cared even less. Let it move out of the way or be trodden into the grass by Mumu and Phoolenda and Alpa and Gulab and… The stampede of death was unstoppable: first over the sock-shaped creature, then the splintering dais, then the scarlet throne and the Gungal Rat, then out into the dark beyond it, until the stars fell down on Kavi – or a spear or an arrow…

"Hee hee hee, can't catch me!
I'm the King of the Elephants, see!"

Gaurang faltered. Mumu collided with her rump, and the cavalcade abruptly slowed. Only then did Kavi realize that the figure on the ground was supposed to be an elephant, too. What is more, it was using the signals of a mahout.

The elephants, confused and nervy, bellowed shrilly, making the crowd scream. Momentum carried their great bulk forward, still forward. The wedding party clutched one another. Some half-rose from their seats, thinking to throw themselves off the dais. Tamburlaine, who never showed fear, simply went on smiling, smiling…

Inside the head of the cloth elephant, Rusti felt sweat roll down his face like tears. *Will you ride me down too, Kavi? Will you?* he said, but not out loud. *Before you kill them, you will have to kill me,* whispered the cloth elephant inside its ridiculous head. Only seconds – only a breath – stood between Rusti and death now. A trunk struck him, a tassle of golden wire swinging from Gaurang's tusk wound itself around his outstretched arm. He reeled, trod back on his trailing elephant bottom, and almost fell.

More of the crowd laughed. A stunt! A show! Of course!

A jumble of trunks flailed the air around and above Rusti's head. He could smell sour hay.

Inside Kavi's head, white tusks of thought slashed to and fro. Why would Rusti try to stop him? Why had Shidurghu moved to sit in the path of the stampede? How would it feel to trample friends in the dirt and hear them die?

Inside the heads of the elephants were greater thoughts by far – thoughts as large and round and silent as the planets in the sky; wordless thoughts made up of instinct and yearning love. Unlike Kavi, they knew Rusti at once. The costume did not fool them. They knew his smell, his voice, his signals. They felt his willpower. Though their foreheads could break down walls, fell towers and trees, they sensed Rusti's willpower, like a wall of glass in the smoky air…

And they would not break it. They came to a halt.

Only Deepti's calf, young, untrained and over-excited, kept on galloping about, knocking over torch-stands and a clutter of drums, crushing the box that had held the doves, toppling a bench full of guests onto their backs. As for the rest, they came to a standstill, nose-to-nose with the wedding guests on the red dais, flakes of purple paint falling like dandruff, speckling the magnificent wedding clothes of the mighty.

Then, one by one, the elephants of Delhi bent a knee to Tamburlaine and his tribe.

Kavi and Rusti looked at one another. Rusti put up a hand and gripped Kavi's ankle. The dust settled. The crowd cheered. Shidurghu crushed the screw of paper between his hands until it was as small as an apple. There were bright spots of colour on his cheeks now, but his expression showed nothing at all. He was unreadable.

"Why?" said Kavi in an undertone. "I help you. You make promise. You help me."

"They would have killed you for it, Kavi. They would have killed you horribly."

"So?"

"The elephants, too."

"Ah," said Kavi.

As if to prove Rusti right, Tamburlaine the Great spoke. Still smiling, still chortling, still nodding his admiration, Tamburlaine spoke out of the corner of his mouth to his Master of Horse and ordered an execution. A bench had been knocked over: some of his guests had been made to look foolish, and that reflected badly on the Emir's hospitality. "Kill it," he said.

Meanwhile Borte, in her slow, dogged and spiteful way had been thinking. The sight of those wretched elephants vexed her past enduring. Their wild stampede around the ring had scared her. The sight of Kavita as a bare-chested boy had baffled her. Anger, fright and bewilderment mixed together inside Borte, dangerous as the ingredients of gunpowder. The sight of her husband emerging from a baggy and ridiculous cloth elephant costume finally lit the fuse. She decided then and there to be rid of this millstone, this embarrassment, this *tajik husband* once and for all. She would inform on him and on the deceitful Kavita who had hoodwinked her.

When she stood up, her head spun: the wedding drink was strong and she had been drinking it as fast as possible to make the most of the Emir's hospitality. Her stomach was bloated, too, from all the bakemeats. She settled the wedding shawl vainly around her shoulders and hurried forwards into the light of the circus ring.

"I know something! I know something you should know, Your Greatness!" Never timid in the first place, liquor made Borte fearless. "That one there! That tajik there – and him..!" she began, moving towards the red dais, pointing, gesticulating.

Two of the Royal Bodyguard seized her by both arms. Standard procedure. No one was suffered to approach the Great Emir – not even members of his own family – unless in the tight grasp of his bodyguards. But Borte did not know that. A stranger to court protocol, she struggled and protested, and the men's grip tightened. "Let go! Get off me! I have to speak to the Emir! I have to tell him about a plot! About that boy there! He's a spy!"

She ought to have waited for the noise to die down. She ought to have waited until the next day when she was sober.

"That Delhi boy there...he's a shape-shifter! He's a girl! And my husband – that tajik – that one there – my husband's brother – he isn't his father's son... I have to tell about the plot!"

The bride and her mother tittered with nervous laughter, but Borte had caught Tamburlaine's attention at last. "Plots" were always of interest to the Emir. He signalled that the bodyguards should bring the woman closer.

Nearby, the Royal Chronicler rose to his feet – frail and pale, a figure of infinite dignity and prestige. Stepping between Borte and the Emir, he said, "Tell me, woman. Is that my wedding shawl you wear around your shoulders? The one that lay in my tent until this morning?"

Startled, Borte squinnied down at the embroidery. "This?"

"For myself, I would give you the coat from my back, if you are in want. Charity is the duty of every man. But to come to a wedding in stolen finery: is that not an insult to your host...and also somewhat foolish?"

Borte's mouth fell open. The bodyguards tightened their grip on her, but their attention was suddenly distracted by a loud squealing. The baby elephant had just met his executioner. The adult elephants shunted each other in alarm. Borte seized her chance and ran. She had been accused of thieving – and by a member of court! She knew what happened to thieves, and Tamburlaine's justice was swift and merciless. Run now, explain later. Outraged innocence was written all over her face, but she bunched up her robe and ran for the darkness – ran for the only break in the circle of gawping faces.

At the same moment, the elephant calf came galloping back in search of its mother, a spear hanging from a wound in its flank, trunk coiled, mouth wide, squealing. It did not notice where it trod or what stood in its path. It barely even noticed the painless collision, the soft obstacle under its feet. As it scrambled and clambered over Borte, its only thought was to reach its mother Deepti, as hers was to reach her calf. Mother and son were reunited in the centre of the circus ring, smudging their purple finery, flank against flank, cheek against cheek, delicately interlacing their trunks, as gently tender as any mother and baby.

The writer-down of History, Shidurghu, was first to reach the side of the trampled woman. He ordered everyone else to stay away, to keep their distance. Reverently he covered the body with the very wedding shawl the thief had stolen from him. Afterwards, he showed everyone the lethal knife he had found (he said) in Borte's hand; told them her dying words too. "The Crooked Pig must die," said Shidurghu, his face a picture of grief and bewilderment. "To me the words make no sense. But I can only guess that she meant to kill the Divine Father of the Nation." And the crowd gasped, suitably horrified.

Tamburlaine granted a reprieve to the elephant calf. In fact, he granted it a royal pardon, and sent his own surgeon to tend the wound his soldiers had made trying to execute it. After all, it had felled an escaping thief – more! – a fleeing assassin.

"I must give her a funeral," said Rusti, still shaking from head to foot.

"You must never speak her name again, or refer to her for as long as you live," said Shidurghu sharply.

"Our glorious Emir has shown the depth of his infinite mercy, or you would be dead already. Generally he puts to death the whole family of those who conspire against him: every cousin, slave, child, horse and dog."

"But she did nothing!"

"Ah!" said the old man, pulling a face. "The worst crime of all, some would say. To live and to do nothing."

They sat facing each other over the chessboard, in a white kibitki lit by a half-dozen candles. There were no pieces on the board. The time for games was past. Rusti would have liked to mourn poor Borte. Instead he felt nothing at all: only a guilty sense of relief, like when thundery weather clears.

Suddenly – like a fortune-teller or a witch – the Chronicler looked clear into Rusti's head and answered the question he found in there.

"Yes, boy, I meant it to be you," he said. "When I first summoned you? During the season of chess? Yes, I intended you to be my accomplice, to do what I could not; to be what I could not." He gave a bitter laugh. "I told you about the tower at Zubihat, thinking you would knock down the man who built it. But you knocked down the tower instead! For that

I blame your mother. There is too much gentleness in you. You take after your mother." He broke off, and his eyes focused not on the Present but on the Past. They had a dull, shineless emptiness, those eyes. He had not been expecting to outlive the Night of the Elephants, and now more years stretched out ahead of him in the service of the man he hated above any other.

"But Kavi was a slave, wasn't he?" suggested Rusti. "So he *had* to do what you told him."

"Aha! Kavi! Free or in chains, Kavi knows nothing but hate. Kavi has a desire as great as mine for revenge." As he spoke, he tapped incessantly with a dry quill on the chessboard. Watching his hand was like seeing a bird dying by degrees.

"Are you my father?"

Shidurghu dropped the quill in surprise. "No! Why? What a thought! What foolish... No! No. Nonsense. Put that vanity out of your head, grubby boy!"

But Rusti did not apologize. "You are a man of Zubihat: the guards told me. You knew my mother. You *are* my father. I've always known! All along! Ever since you drew the tower!"

"NO!"

Rusti slumped back in his chair so heavily that it almost overturned. He had wanted it so much to be true – wondered if he could go on pretending, even now, because he wanted it so much to be true.

"No. No, no, no." Shidurghu fumbled in his pocket, took out a single coin, clicked it down on the chessboard. Again the coin. "What does it say?"

Rusti picked up the coin and said in bored disgust, "*Rasti and Rusti.* I can't read it, but everyone knows that. 'Truth and Safety'."

Shidurghu nodded. His whole body seemed to be settling like a bonfire after the fire has burned out its heart. "The father who named you could have chosen either word: 'Rasti' or 'Rusti'. 'Truth' or 'Safety'. He chose 'Safety'. Think, boy. He chose 'Safety'. That was what he wished for you. Who am I to thwart him in his wishes? Baliq was a wise man. Who can live with the Truth in his heart without his heart breaking?"

"Baliq wasn't my father! The man who took me and left my mother in the tower? The man who called me Rusti? He was a Mongol. That's all *he* was."

Shidurghu banged the table. Alerted by the sudden noise, a guard ducked his head inside the tent to see that no harm had come to the Royal Chronicler. When he had gone again, Shidurghu lowered his voice to a whisper: a shouted whisper that whistled in his throat. "That Mongol gave you life when you had none! Baliq gave you a place at his hearth! He fed and clothed you. These are the things a father does. Not all Mongols are bad. That much my years of captivity have taught me. Some are good men. The man who took you into his family was a good man.

"Me, I *watch*. Oh I am a great *watcher*. That is my *Fate*, you see boy. While men around me fight and die and rejoice and marry and live and suffer and sing, what does Shidurghu do? Shidurghu holds still and *watches*, like a man watching fish in a pool!

"Just once I was tempted, it is true. I gave in to temptation. 'A game of chess: what hurt is there in that?' I said to myself. 'A horse for the boy: what harm? Teach him to read! (Try, at least.) Save the fool of a boy from the danger he is putting himself in with this Delhi boy…!' Just once I reached out… And you see the result? The water splashed. The fish scattered. I am left looking only into darkness. I wanted to make an assassin out of you, boy, but your mother's spirit prevented me. I will not make the same mistake again. I will hold still: as still as a man in his grave!"

His whispering – his huge, raging whisper – made the old man's chest heave and the hollows of his throat deepen and the veins throb in his forehead. He reached for a jug of mare's milk, but Rusti poured it for him instead.

"I can still come here. We can still play chess!"

"No."

It felt like being kicked. "I would help you. Next time. Another time. I would! I would!"

"I have said all the words that need to be said. Go."

But Rusti did not go. "You didn't breathe," he said, and Shidurghu frowned, not understanding. "You told me once to think for the space of one breath before I decided on a move."

The Chronicler gave an impatient wave of his hand and turned his face away. Rusti was dismissed.

But Rusti took a long deep breath and waited, feeling the fragrant smoke from the candle coil and twist inside him like ghosts in a tower. "I have decided, Your Honour," he said. "I have decided on my move. I mean to be a tajik. A stayer-in-one-place. I will stay here in Samarqand."

Shidurghu nodded impatiently, in a hurry for Rusti to leave. But Rusti had not finished. He went to the desk, took up a sheet of parchment and a pen, and laid them on the chessboard. "Draw," he said.

The old man gripped the arms of his chair as if he

was about to get up. "The tower again? No. I will not."

"No," said Rusti. "Not the tower. Draw my mother."

The look on Shidurghu's face said that the task was beyond him, impossible, out of the question, unthinkable. But he did take up the pen and he did draw. For a time the only sound was the scratching of the pen and their breathing settling into the same rhythm.

A glimmer of wet ink; a sprinkling of white sand to dry it, and the parchment changed hands. Only then did Rusti turn his back and make for the door.

After the space of, say, one breath, and just as Rusti lifted the flap of the tent, the old man spoke:

"In all the years since Zubihat, not one breath has passed out of me but I have thought of my daughter. Walled up inside that tower. And of her child. Her little boy."

Then Rusti turned and kneeled and pressed his forehead to the soft plush of the carpet, and the sun caught on a coin, as he laid it down at arm's length in front of him. Circling it, he laid a gold O – a woman's bracelet.

"Be safe, honoured grandfather. The Truth is safe with me."

Chapter Fourteen

Two Years On...

Rusti sits on a plain called the Rose-mine, outside Samarqand, capital of Tamburlaine's Empire. Around him, like humps of earth left by a gravedigger, lie the captured elephants of Delhi. Tonight, they will parade in honour of the Emir's new wife, the twelve-year-old Taman-aghan whom he married yesterday in among the gorgeous pavilions of fur and silk that sprinkle the Rose-mine. The elephants will bend their knees respectfully. They will stretch their trunks and bellow a trumpet fanfare in celebration of the happy event. There will be a circus and poetry, feasting and an ocean of drink.

Rusti has also married again – a sweet girl from Tashkent, whom he heard singing one day outside his window. All nationalities live in Samarqand; where they were born matters very little. His wife Ghazal does not ride into battle, a blue silk sash across her face and only her scowl showing. She is not a warrior. But then neither is Rusti. City men cannot hope to marry fighting wives. Ghazal's delight is in breeding foals from Arrow. She made Rusti buy a pretty brood mare which cost him all of Borte's loot and more. He did not mind in the least, but the fact remains: marriage is still a day-to-day terror for Rusti. This wife is so delightful that he cannot quite believe she will stay – that she will not simply wander off one day. He cannot quite believe that Ghazal loves him for anything but his horses.

Little does he know that Ghazal lives in fear and trembling, too. In the tiny family apartment hangs a pen-and-ink portrait of the most beautiful woman she has ever seen. Thinking it must be Rusti's dead wife (whom he never, never mentions), Ghazal cannot imagine how she can possibly comfort him for such a loss, how she herself can possibly compare with such a beauty.

In one way, though, she is like Borte. Ghazal is afraid of elephants. So whenever Rusti goes to the zoo and sits with his animals and talks to them of God and lightning and India, he goes there alone. They regard him sorrowfully with their small eyes, nod their great heads in sorrowful understanding, caress his face sympathetically with the fluted ends of their trunks. *We understand*, they seem to say. *We too have been enslaved by someone smaller than ourselves*. He loves them too: his elephant confidantes, loves to lie along their bony spines on a night like this, counting the stars.

Inside Samarqand today there were silk banners in the streets and red apples floating in the public fountains. There was a royal hunting expedition with greyhounds and panthers, a polo tournament, and a reading of poetry. Rusti's head is aswirl with the memory of it.

But though the wedding festivities will last for weeks, he knows Emir Tamburlaine will not stay. He never does. Cities are for tajiks. Soon the kibitkis and pavilions and travelling mosques will be packed onto carts again, and a new campaign will begin. The Lord of the Fortunate Conjunction will lead his million-strong family out again on their perpetual journey of conquest...

Two Years On...

Not Rusti. Rusti works now at the royal mint in Samarqand, striking coins which carry three planets and three words. Throughout Tamburlaine's vast Empire, these coins pay for everything: bread and slaves and swords and bracelets and spies and paper and ink and towers of brick. The coins Rusti makes will travel as far as the edge of the world…but Rusti will stay at home.

Only at times like these, when the Horde reels home full of drink and loot and stories and scars and boasting and contempt, only then do the royal elephants come into their own again. As the acrobats string their tightropes and the clowns sew themselves into their animal costumes…then Rusti parades his real-life elephants out of Samarqand, onto the Rose-mine, to perform in the royal circuses.

Tamburlaine's finest cavalrymen gallop their horses up and down, performing death-defying feats. They pick up their shields from the ground without ever leaving the saddle. They shoot their arrows into targets while riding at full gallop. They slice the heads from straw dummies and send them rolling in among the feet of the crowd who bray like donkeys, with delight. But sadly Rusti is a tajik. So all he sees, as the straw head rolls to a halt between his feet, is a soft cheek, a beardless chin, a pair of eyes asking him a question he cannot answer.

No matter. A boy astride an elephant is taller than any warrior, and Rusti parades the elephants of Samarqand out onto the Rose-mine, to perform in the royal circuses.

He and Kavi, that is. For where would the elephants of Delhi be without their mahout? And where would Rusti be without his best friend?

Mumu lifts her trunk and snuffs the scent of roses, spices, feasting. She looks as if she is groping for the stars. But the boys know better. They know that elephants ask very little from life. Only Tamburlaine is ambitious to capture the stars and all the lands that lie beneath them.

Author's Note

Timur i Lang (1336–1404) became ruler of Transoxania – a huge empire encompassing a vast tract of Central Asia. He set out to conquer Persia, northern India, the Ottomans and Malmuks, and China. There is no such place as Zubihat, but there were many like it visited by the Emir on his endless travels. In Western history books – and Christopher Marlowe's famous play – Timur i Lang is referred to as "Tamburlaine the Great".

Geraldine McCaughrean is "a superb storyteller"

Times Educational Supplement

A Conversation with Geraldine McCaughrean

What was your inspiration for writing *Tamburlaine's Elephants*?

I have always loved the work of the Elizabethan playwright Christopher Marlowe. He shoved his plays together with all the finesse of someone stuffing a cushion, but the poetry he used was just fabulous. He even managed to make Tamburlaine pitiable at a couple of moments in the play just by putting such beautiful words into his mouth. When I read up on the real thing, though, Timur i Lang did not have any redeeming qualities. He was just a brutish despot. But that was okay, because I wanted to write a book about two boys caught up in Timur's world, not about the man himself.

The shifting, rootless existence of the Mongol Horde fascinates me, too. It is a bit like modern society, always wanting to move on, get somewhere else, gain some new ground; never content to come to a halt and rest easy.

Why does writing historical fiction appeal to you, and how much research do you do?

I have always liked writing about The Past: it is the one holiday resort no travel agent can take you to but a book can. And life was so much more dangerous and life-threatening six centuries ago. I admit, I never used to do much historical research before setting to work on a new book. If my book was set in medieval England I would simply steer clear of including cars and nylon and TV... I was not, after all, setting out to educate my readers. (Don't you just loathe those books that digress from the plot to tell you a little bit about Norman architecture or the causes of the Peasants' Revolt?) But then I started writing adult books, and adults, unlike young readers, mind very much if an author gets her facts wrong: they write in and complain and you have to write back and apologize. So it was that I discovered the joys of historical research! Such amazing, bizarre things happened in the past! Things I could never make up in a hundred years.

The only problem is that if an author has compiled a whole card-file full of interesting facts, there is a temptation to try and cram them all into the book, and that can slow down the action. So now I tend to throw the card-file out of the window after a chapter or two.

And it never hurts to make things up, either. This is fiction we are talking about, after all. My mother once said, about a book I had written that was set in a French chateau, "I could tell which bits were based on things you saw while you were in France." But when she described those scenes, they were all things I had invented myself.

Where do you get your ideas?

I usually base a story on some crumb of true fact – something I have read in the newspaper (*Gold Dust*); some documentary I have seen on TV (*Stop the Train*), or some passing mention in a book (*Plundering Paradise*). I have retold a lot of myths during my career, so myths often creep into my stories, too. I am forever looking for subjects that no one has ever written about before. This is really stupid of me. Clever authors find one sort of book that they can do well and which pleases their readers, then stick with it. Series books sell very well. But I have never written a sequel to any of my books. The only sequel I have ever written was to someone else's book – J. M. Barrie's *Peter Pan and Wendy*. But my mum told me "Never boil your cabbages twice, dear", so I don't. I want each new book to turn out differently from anything I've ever done before. Anyway, that's half the fun – giving myself a new challenge. Mind you, *Tamburlaine's Elephants* is in fact my second book involving the Mongol Empire. *The Kite Rider* was set in China at the time when the Mongol Khubilah Khan had conquered it and made it part of his vast empire...but that was a long time before Timur i Lang came along.

Have you always been a writer?
I did a lot of jobs – secretary, teacher, journalist, sub-editor. But I wrote as I travelled to and from work: it was my hobby. Now I stay home all day and write. It's great, but it still seems odd to earn a living by having so much fun.

What or who initially inspired you to start to write?
I have a very clever older brother called Neil. When I was young, everything he did, I wanted to do. So when, at 14, he had a book published, that became a great ambition of mine. I was also very shy and timid. (I still am.) The one place I dared to have adventures was in my imagination, writing stories.

What is your favourite book?
As a child I remember enjoying *The Ship that Flew* by

Hilda Lewis as well as horsey books like *Silver Brumby* and historical novels by Rosemary Sutcliffe. I think now that Alan Ahlberg's *Jeremiah in the Dark Woods* is literally "perfect" – not a word wrong, not a comma out of place. My favourite adult books get inside the heads of each character in turn and make you like and understand every single one.

What is your favourite place?
Home, definitely, though I do like hot sun and blue-sea-side and bright, bright light. I get gloomy in the winter.

Do you have any pets at home?
Daisy, a Golden Retriever. Until recently we had never had pets – except for fan-tail doves which the neighbourhood cats quickly ate.

What ambitions do you still have?
I'd like to write more plays – for stage and radio and schools. Maybe *Peter Pan in Scarlet* will give me the chance. I'd like to get on a train or tube or bus and see the passenger opposite reading a book of mine. One day!

GERALDINE McCAUGHREAN is one of today's most successful and highly regarded children's authors. She has won the Carnegie Medal, the Whitbread Children's Book Award (three times), the Guardian Children's Fiction Prize, the Smarties Bronze Award (four times) and the Blue Peter Book of the Year Award. In 2005 she was chosen from over 100 other authors to write the official sequel to J. M. Barrie's *Peter Pan*. *Peter Pan in Scarlet* was published in 2006 to wide critical acclaim.

Geraldine lives in Berkshire with her husband, daughter and golden retriever, Daisy.

www.geraldinemccaughrean.co.uk

Usborne Quicklinks

For links to websites where you can learn more about the Mighty Tamburlaine and the famous battles he led, and find out what it was like to live a nomadic life with the Horde, go to the Usborne Quicklinks Website at www.usborne-quicklinks.com and enter the keywords "tamburlaine's elephants".

Internet safety

When using the internet, make sure you follow these safety guidelines:

- Ask an adult's permission before using the internet.
- Never give out personal information, such as your name, address or telephone number.
- If a website asks you to type in your name or e-mail address, check with an adult first.
- If you receive an e-mail from someone you don't know, don't reply to it.